THE

HUGO
MOVIE
COMPANION

THE
HUGO
MOVIE
COMPANION

A Behind the Scenes Look at How a Beloved Book
Became a Major Motion Picture

BY BRIAN SELZNICK

With additional material by
Martin Scorsese and David Serlin

PHOTOGRAPHY BY JAAP BUITENDIJK

SCHOLASTIC PRESS • NEW YORK

This book is dedicated to
Martin, Helen, and Francesca Scorsese

Published by Scholastic Press, an imprint of Scholastic Inc.,
Publishers since 1920. SCHOLASTIC, SCHOLASTIC PRESS,
and associated logos are trademarks
and/or registered trademarks of Scholastic Inc.

Library of Congress Cataloging-in-Publication Data available
ISBN 978-0-545-33155-5
10 9 8 7 6 5 4 3 2 1   11 12 13 14 15
Printed in Singapore   46
First edition, October 2011

This book was designed by
Brian Selznick, Charles Kreloff, and David Saylor.

CONTENTS

A BRIEF INTRODUCTION

THE STORY I AM ABOUT TO SHARE WITH YOU takes place in London, Paris, New York, and Los Angeles, with brief stops in New Jersey, Italy, Canada, Aruba, and a hundred other locations. You will hear about clocks and train stations, complicated automatons and brilliant actors, as well as the latest in cutting-edge technology, some old-fashioned magic, and a legendary film director or two. You will visit graveyards and toy shops, theaters, libraries, and secret rooms hidden behind walls. You will meet a boy named Asa Butterfield, who once, not that long ago, found out he was going to play Hugo in a movie of the same name. You'll learn about the great glass film studio of Georges Méliès, which fell to ruins in France many years ago and was rebuilt in England in 2010.

All of this and more was inspired by my book, *The Invention of Hugo Cabret*, where Méliès, speaking of that glass studio, says, "If you've ever wondered where your dreams come from when you go to sleep at night, just look around. This is where they are made."

Follow me now and I'll show you how a book was created, a movie was made, and a dream was born.

Brian Selznick

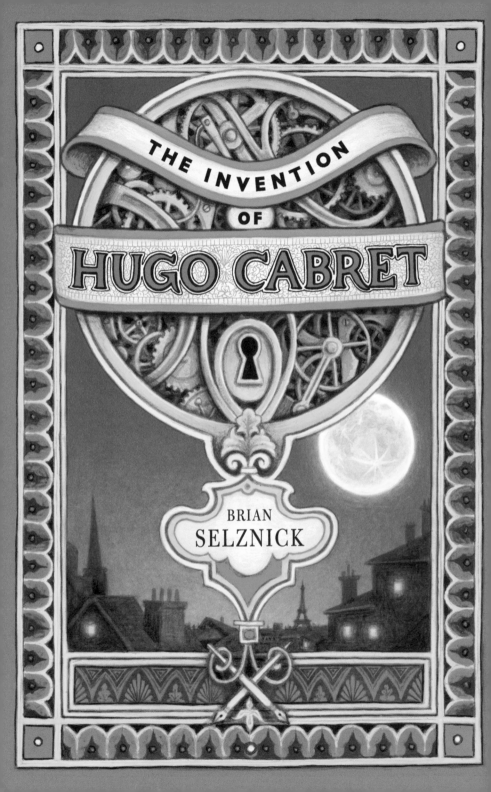

CHAPTER ONE

THE ORIGINAL BOOK

A scene from A Trip to the Moon
directed by Georges Méliès,
which was inspiration for
The Invention of Hugo Cabret.

A Trip to the Moon

It all began with *A Trip to the Moon*. I can't remember exactly when I first saw the mesmerizing 1902 film by Georges Méliès, but I was very young. I grew up in East Brunswick, New Jersey, the oldest of three kids. I loved to draw and watch monster movies. My grandfather's first cousin was the famous film producer David O. Selznick, who made the original *King Kong*, as well as *Gone with the Wind*, *Duel in the Sun*, and many other classic movies. He and my grandfather grew up together, and even though they both died before I was born, my grandmother's house was filled with books about David O. Selznick that I loved to read. Perhaps this is why I've always loved movies.

At some point I saw *A Trip to the Moon*, and the rocket that flew into the eye of the man in the moon lodged itself firmly in my imagination. I wanted to write a story about a kid who meets Méliès, but I didn't know what the plot would be. The years passed. I wrote and illustrated over twenty other books. Then, sometime in 2003, I happened to pick up a book called *Edison's Eve* by Gaby Wood. It's a history of automatons, and to my surprise, one chapter was about Méliès. I learned that he had owned a collection of automatons that were donated to a museum at the end of his life. The museum put them in the attic, where they were all destroyed by rain and thrown away. I instantly imagined a boy climbing through the garbage and finding one of those broken machines. I didn't know who the boy was at first, and I didn't even know his name. But I remembered a toy I loved as a kid called "Hugo, the Man of a Thousand Faces," and I thought the name *Hugo* sounded kind of French. The only other French word I could think of was *cabaret*, and I thought that *Cabret* might sound like a real French name. *Voilà* . . . Hugo Cabret was born.

For inspiration during the two and a half years I created the book, I watched many hours of French movies, especially those from the 1920s and '30s. I discovered directors like Jean Vigo, René Clair, and Jean Renoir (the son of the great impressionist painter Pierre-Auguste Renoir). Because my story is centered around a filmmaker (and maybe because of my relationship to David O. Selznick), I wanted to experiment with the visual aspect of my story. I decided to tell part of the story in images, *like a movie.* I returned to my manuscript and removed as much text as I could, replacing words with illustrated sequences so we could *watch* those parts of the story. For instance, there's a scene where Hugo is following a mysterious old man as they leave the train station where Hugo is living. As they walk through the streets, the old man says to himself, "I hope the snow covers everything so all the footsteps are silenced, and the whole city can be at peace." We then turn the page and watch as the rest of their journey unfolds. . . .

I also began learning more about automatons, and eventually made my way to the Franklin Institute in Philadelphia. There, in storage, was a two-hundred-year-old automaton built by Henri Maillardet, in the shape of a man sitting at a desk. It had broken many years earlier, and no one at the time was sure how to fix it. My friend Andy Baron, a mechanical genius, was invited to repair the machine, and now it's working like new again. Andy taught me all about clocks and gears, and he described himself when he was a child like Hugo, taking apart and fixing whatever machines he could find. He told me how he'd tilt his head to one side so he could listen to the machine, making sure everything sounded just right. With Andy's permission, I gave details like this to Hugo as he went about trying desperately to fix his father's broken automaton.

While I studied automatons, I also traveled three times to Paris. I wanted to immerse myself in the city where my story would take place. I started by visiting all the train stations in the city (including one that has been transformed into a famous museum, the Musée d'Orsay; I borrowed two of their clocks for my book). The stations were built in the nineteenth century with grand staircases, ornate columns, pointed glass roofs, palm trees in huge pots, sculptures, elaborate façades, and, of course, huge clocks everywhere. The station where Méliès worked, the Gare Montparnasse (*gare* means "train station" in French), is the only one that has been torn down, so to create the train station in my book, I used vintage photographs of the original station, as well as bits and pieces from many other stations in Paris, especially the Gare du Nord. I also used details from Grand Central Terminal in New York City because I once heard that there are secret rooms above the starry ceiling in the main concourse. That's what gave me the idea for Hugo's secret apartment behind the walls.

With a little detective work, I was able to track down the original apartment building where Méliès lived, so the corresponding picture in my book is accurate. On my last visit to Paris, right before the book came out, I found Méliès's grave at the famous cemetery, Père-Lachaise. Standing there, with the history of the City of Light echoing all around me, I made a little card for Méliès. On the front, I drew a pen and ink sketch of the rocket in the eye of the man in the moon. Beneath the moon, I wrote: *From a fan in America*, and inside: *Thank you.*

The Gare du Nord (North Station) in Paris, France.

Drawing of the interior of the train station from The Invention of Hugo Cabret.

Giant clock in the Musée d'Orsay, a museum in Paris that was built in an old train station.

WHAT WAS PARIS REALLY LIKE IN 1931?

by David Serlin

The Eiffel Tower

The city of Paris has long been celebrated in poems, songs, books, and movies. But in 1931 it was still recovering from the devastation of World War I and dealing with the same hardships that had swept the United States and many other parts of the world during the Great Depression. The rise of political figures, like Adolf Hitler in Germany and Benito Mussolini in Italy, caused great uncertainty about the future of Europe. Still, 1931 proved to be an important year for the French capital.

One of the major events of 1931 was a popular fairground and museum complex known as the International Colonial Exposition. Exhibits featured re-creations of buildings and gardens as well as examples of food, clothing, music, and local culture from the many nations France ruled over, such as Vietnam, Haiti, Algeria, Senegal, and parts of China. These countries, and others, were "colonies" of France, which is why the event was called the International Colonial Exposition. After the exposition closed, some of the buildings were dismantled and reassembled in other parts of France. Many of them still stand today.

That same year, the director René Clair released the movie *A nous la liberté* (*Freedom for Us*), which was so popular with US audiences that it was the first foreign film to be nominated for an Academy Award, in the category of Best Art Direction.

Cinema had become extremely popular and its influence was everywhere, especially in fashion. Common people wanted to look like movie stars, even as the stars in movies were often trying to look like common people. Despite economic hardship, men and women, wanting to look stylish, wore hats and gloves. Boys wore knickers that buttoned at the knee, and girls wore long dresses. Women plucked their eyebrows into very fine lines and shaped their nails into short oval points. Many men grew little mustaches; short hairstyles were the fashion.

Music filled the air in Paris in 1931. Romantic and patriotic songs were performed live by singers in restaurants and night-clubs called *cabarets*. But because it could be expensive to go out for an evening's entertainment, many Parisians listened to pho-nograph records at home. On the radio they could hear popular music by people like Stéphane Grappelli or Django Reinhardt.

During this time, many people in France debated what Paris would look like in the years to come. The famous architect Le Corbusier, for example, proposed a grid of skyscrapers that would either stand beside Paris's more famous buildings or com-pletely replace them. These discussions took place at the height of the artistic movement known as *Art Deco*, which proposed that all designed objects, from buildings to cars to clothes to jewelry, look futuristic. But the designs were often inspired by Egyptian forms, like pyramids. This sometimes gave the impression that Parisians were living in the ancient past and the distant future at the same time.

Paris in 1931. On the left you can see Gustave Eiffel's famous tower (built for the Universal Exhibition of 1889) looming over the many apartment buildings and wide boulevards on the Right Bank. The Eiffel Tower was the tallest structure in the world until 1930 when the Chrysler Building in New York City surpassed it.

Director Martin Scorsese, wearing his 3-D glasses,
stands on a re-creation of a set by Georges Méliès.

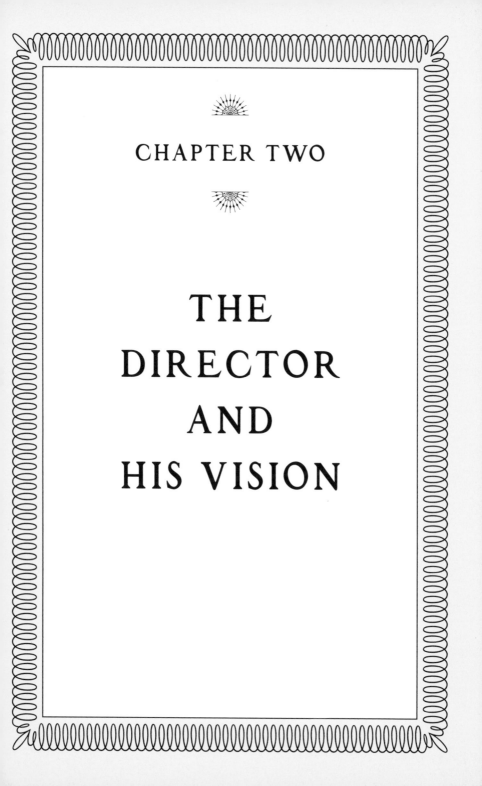

CHAPTER TWO

THE DIRECTOR AND HIS VISION

Martin Scorsese

DIRECTOR

Martin Scorsese explains that the job of a director is to do "the same thing that children do when they play . . . make up stories, give people parts to play, and figure out where they go and what they do. Others compare the job to that of a conductor or painter . . . it's all the same. The key is to figure out how to tell the story *with pictures*: a person's face, or a landscape, or an object. And how to frame that face, landscape, or object in order to communicate the narrative, the emotion."

Scorsese has made some of the greatest movies of all time, and he's worked closely with child actors before. "It doesn't matter what age an actor is. What's important is the ability to understand a scene, a concept, the truth of a situation. If they get it, they get it."

Soon after *The Invention of Hugo Cabret* was published, a copy landed on Scorsese's desk. "I was attracted to the character of Hugo and his predicament. I was attracted to the atmosphere in which he lives, and drawn into the mystery of the automaton.

"The mechanical objects in the film, including cameras, projectors, and automatons, make it possible for Hugo to reconnect with his father. And mechanical objects make it possible for the filmmaker Georges

Méliès to reconnect with his past, and with himself.

"To prepare to make a movie from *The Invention of Hugo Cabret*, I met with the whole creative team to discuss costumes, makeup, set design, props, and so on, with historical photographs and films as reference. The objective was to create our own universe with its own visual language. We wanted to find a balance between realism and myth. This is partially expressed in visual details such as the color of a costume or the placement and size of a poster. The Paris we created has a basis in reality but it is not an exact reproduction."

As a kid growing up in New York City's Little Italy in the 1940s and '50s, Scorsese says he "felt a passion for the movies. It was sparked by my obsession with the illusion of movement that motion pictures create. *The Invention of Hugo Cabret* tapped into that obsession. It connects with the psychological and emotional impact of those images and how I related them to myself and those around me, my family. In a sense, the same thing happens to Hugo. There is a similarity to my other films because at the heart of *The Invention of Hugo Cabret* is a story about a father and son. Many of my other films deal with this. I related to Hugo and his father going to the movies together. My father often took me to see movies when I was a child. The movie theater was a special place for us. It was a time for us to be alone and to share powerful emotional experiences together."

Martin Scorsese (age five) in 1947, with his parents, Charles and Catherine, in Corona, Queens, before they moved to Little Italy. Around this time, Scorsese saw his very first movie, David O. Selznick's Duel in the Sun.

DAVID O. SELZNICK
The Producer Who Gave You
"GONE WITH THE WIND"
Presents
DUEL
in the SUN
in Technicolor
starring JENNIFER JONES
GREGORY PECK · JOSEPH COTTEN
with
LIONEL BARRYMORE · HERBERT MARSHALL · LILLIAN GISH
WALTER HUSTON · CHARLES BICKFORD · WITH A CAST OF 2500
Directed by KING VIDOR
A Selznick Re-release

In 1931, the new technology of sound was regarded with suspicion by many people who thought it was just a gimmick. Today there is a similar feeling regarding 3-D. Directors like René Clair helped revolutionize the way people thought about sound, and now Scorsese is helping revolutionize the thinking about 3-D. This new technology can change the way stories are understood on screen. Scorsese says 3-D "offers a profound sense of space for each area that Hugo inhabits. It enhances the contrast between the vast interior of the train station and the narrow tunnels through which Hugo travels, and the different clocks he winds. It also provides a real sense of space *inside* the clocks — especially the tower clock. In 3-D, you get a sense of the *power* of those mechanisms. In 2-D, I would have lost the sense of scale and particularly that of perspective. In 3-D, the depth within the frame distances Hugo in such a way that makes him stronger and braver. He's up against so much. Gears and mechanisms large and small mark off moments in his life. And we're all measured in life by time. 3-D makes this point much stronger.

"Probably the first images I saw in my head when I began working on this were images of Hugo running and looking over his shoulder, and there was a longing in his eyes. Faces are given a special intimacy with 3-D. We see people in a different way. They are closer to us. I felt that

3-D would help create a stronger bond between the audience and the characters."

Since 3-D brings us into Hugo's world in a special way, Scorsese felt that the world itself had to be created with great care. "*The Invention of Hugo Cabret* takes place in Paris in 1931. Now, in our movie everyone is speaking English and the story is magical. But I wanted to capture the feeling of Paris at that time. A strong sense of time and place is important when you're telling stories. In order for something fantastic or magical to find its power, it has to be set against something ordinary and easily believable. So it was our job to create a world for our story. And because this story is about the relationship between a boy and a moviemaker in France, I looked for some of my inspiration to the French movies of the early 1930s, like those by Jean Renoir, Jean Vigo, and René Clair. Their movies gave me a way of thinking about France during that time: the people, the places, the atmosphere, the sense of beauty.

"I also talked a lot about the film with my youngest daughter, Francesca, after she had read the book. We talked about her feelings toward Hugo and about Isabelle and her love of literature. We talked about the automaton and how it was very special. Francesca asked me many, many questions. She was very curious *how* we were going to turn *The Invention of Hugo Cabret* into a film. . . ."

Martin Scorsese, wearing his clip-on 3-D glasses, discusses a scene from the original book with Asa Butterfield (Hugo) and Chloë Moretz (Isabelle).

Martin Scorsese and cinematographer
Robert Richardson discuss a shot on
the monitor of the 3-D cameras.

Chloë Moretz (Isabelle) and Asa Butterfield (Hugo) listen carefully as Martin Scorsese gives them directions for a scene.

Christopher Lee (Monsieur Labisse)
and Martin Scorsese discuss a scene
in Labisse's bookstore.

Martin Scorsese welcomes Jude Law (Hugo's father) to the set. This scene was filmed in the Victoria and Albert Museum in London, England.

THE BIRTH OF CINEMA

by Martin Scorsese

The Lumière Brothers

The art of cinema, which many of us refer to as "the movies," began in the mid-1890s. The pioneers were inventors *and* entertainers, and they discovered something wondrous: the illusion of motion. You could say that this was a historical process, beginning with painting, moving a giant step forward with photography, and ending with cinema. And it happened first in France, in 1895, to be exact. Two brothers perfected a process in which multiple still photographs were taken every second with a hand-cranked camera, and then projected at the same rate of speed on a screen. It's fitting that the brothers were named Lumière, because that's the French word for "light," as precious to the cinema as oxygen is to human life.

Auguste and Louis Lumière made hundreds of films that lasted only a few minutes each, but I still find them exciting to watch, because they unfold with the thrill of discovery. How did it feel to be the first filmmakers, to capture the movements of a baby with its parents, of workers leaving a factory, of a train arriving at a station? And when you watch these films, you are there with them, back at the beginning. The Lumières thought that the movies were a novelty, a passing fad, but what they had actually created was a whole new way of experiencing and interpreting the world — a new art form.

Motion and emotion. They were, and are, at the core of cinema. And it was Georges Méliès who provided the final key element: magic. In fact, Méliès *was* a magician, and he saw moving pictures as a way to enrich and enlarge his stage presentations. In so doing, he took the movies another giant step forward. The Lumières gave us the world as we knew it, and Méliès gave it to us as we imagined and extended it, with imaginary voyages, disappearances, and transformations.

The French have always had a special relationship with cinema, and the history of French moviemaking is a long and glorious one, continuing through the silent era with masters like Louis Feuillade and Jean Epstein, then flourishing at the dawn of sound with Jean Vigo, René Clair, and the incomparable Jean Renoir, then later with great artists like Jean Cocteau, Jean-Pierre Melville, Robert Bresson, and the filmmakers of the New Wave of the 1950s and '60s like François Truffaut and Alain Resnais and Jean-Luc Godard, who took the cinema to bold new places that no one in 1895 could even have begun to imagine.

But it all began with the Lumière Brothers and with Georges Méliès. All of us who make movies owe them a debt

L'Eclipse (The Eclipse), 1907, *directed by Georges Méliès.*

L'Arrivée d'un train á La Ciotat (Arrival of a Train at La Ciotat), *1895, by the Lumière Brothers. This is one of the first films ever made.*

Sous les toits de Paris (Under the Roofs of Paris), *1930, directed by René Clair.*

La belle et la bête (Beauty and the Beast), 1946, directed by Jean Cocteau.

Les quatre cents coups (The 400 Blows), 1959, directed by François Truffaut.

Marianne Bower

RESEARCHER

Marianne Bower says her job is to take care of Martin
Scorsese's paper archives, which contain letters, scripts,
drawings, photos, and files generated when one of his
films is made. "I am also asked to do research or find
books or music or other information related to possible
future projects."

As a child in Chappaqua, New York, Marianne loved
to ask people about their past. "I liked hearing about
how people lived long ago, and I liked hearing how they
told their stories. I particularly liked hearing about the
details of their lives that might be different from my own.
One of the first movies I ever saw as a child was *Oliver!* I
could relate to the energy of the children, but I was also
excited to be experiencing something from the past. I
loved feeling immersed in history, as if I were time travel-
ing." When she grew up, one of Marianne's first jobs was
finding visual research for a documentary on TV. "I
really liked the detective work that research sometimes
requires." For *Hugo*, Marianne says, "I started by making a list of the locations in the script and looking for as
many photos and illustrations of those locations as I
could find within a very specific time frame: 1925 to
1931. I collected as many books and documentaries as I
could find about Georges Méliès and his films. Marty

looked at all of this material and then gave instructions as to which actor or designer was to get what. I also looked for automatons in action to show Marty. I came across Michael Start's amazing website (automatomania.co.uk), which has several videos of automatons from the nineteenth century. I made a compilation DVD, including the Franklin Institute automaton mentioned in Brian's book, for Marty and others to look at."

One of the stranger things Marianne was asked to locate was a photograph for the Station Inspector's office, which would recall the character's time in the army during World War I. "Scorsese mentioned a movie that had a scene with horses in gas masks in it. David Balfour, the props master, said that dogs wore gas masks in World War I, too. Because the Inspector has such a close relationship with his dog, I looked for photos of dogs wearing gas masks. As luck would have it, I found a photo of a French World War I soldier with his dog on a leash, both of them wearing gas masks. It is an odd photo that seems at home in the Inspector's office amidst all of his other paraphernalia.

"For every project, I usually make a stop at the Picture Collection of the New York Public Library just to get my bearings. I make binders for myself, categorized by location or character type. For example: cafés, train stations, home interiors, train personnel, policemen, etc. I try to keep everything as organized as possible so it is easy to find and copy for anyone who may find it useful."

Brassaï's photo of an old police station in Paris, 1930.

Brassaï's photo of a Paris street, 1932.

André Kertész's photo of a Parisian bistro, 1927.

A Parisian street corner built on a soundstage for *Hugo, inspired by photographs on the facing page. Lights are hung from scaffolding. White cloths help enclose the set and keep out daylight.*

RUE
DE DOMINIQUE

38 · COM^ce de VINS

J·LAURANS

CIDRE
60

Vin 60

GROS
ET
A

RE-CREATING MÉLIÈS

with Martin Scorsese and Marianne Bower

Martin Scorsese (left), viewed through a reproduction of Méliès's fish tank.

"It would have been extraordinary to have been a part of creating the first movies," says Martin Scorsese. "Filming the flashback scenes in *Hugo* is perhaps as close as I'll ever get to experiencing that. Méliès's films have an exuberance, joy, and excitement I associate with the actual creation of this new art form and I wanted to capture that." According to Marianne Bower, every department watched Méliès's films and painstakingly re-created the sets, costumes, and props. "The name of the Méliès film being re-created in *Hugo* is *Kingdom of the Fairies* from 1903. This was for the scene when we see the professor, René Tabard, as a young boy meeting Méliès for the first time. The specific moment is when the Lobster Guards (as we called them) lead a procession to Neptune, where the hero begs Neptune to be released back home — at least I think that's what he's doing!"

Méliès's original glass studio was rebuilt on the backlot of

Shepperton Studios in England where most of the film was shot, using existing designs, measurements, and photos of the original building. The scenery was painted in tones of gray, as it was originally, and the props department built or refurbished workable period cameras. "Marty studied photos of Méliès and crew working at the studio to get an idea of the kinds of activity that would be going on while Méliès is shooting the scene," Marianne says. "The costume designer had discussions with Marty about the color of the costumes since there was conflicting information about whether or not Méliès always used black-and-white costumes. The Cinémathèque Française has a few original costumes that are full color." The makeup designer said that no red was used because on the old film stock it would have looked black. Beards, wigs, and lobster-headed costumes and claws were all based on careful viewings of the scene.

Marianne adds, "In order to create the illusion that the scene is taking place under the sea, Méliès (and Scorsese) shot through a large fish tank. Lobsters were thrown into the tank to complete the illusion. Of interest is that Méliès had to place the fish tank at the correct distance from the action and from the camera so that the fish didn't look too large or too small in comparison with the actors. There is a drawing depicting this ratio in the Cinémathèque Française, which was consulted by the special effects and camera crews."

Scorsese says, "As a moviemaker, I feel that we owe everything to Georges Méliès. And when I go back and look at his original films, I feel moved and inspired, because they carry the thrill of discovery over one hundred years after they were made; and because they are among the first, powerful expressions of an art form that I've loved, and to which I've devoted myself for the better part of my life."

The 3-D cameras approach the re-creation of Méliès's glass film studio, as actors playing the young Tabard and his brother walk toward the entrance.

Diagram from the Cinémathèque Française, used by Scorsese's team, showing the exact placement for the fish tank and the camera in order to achieve the illusion of filming underwater.

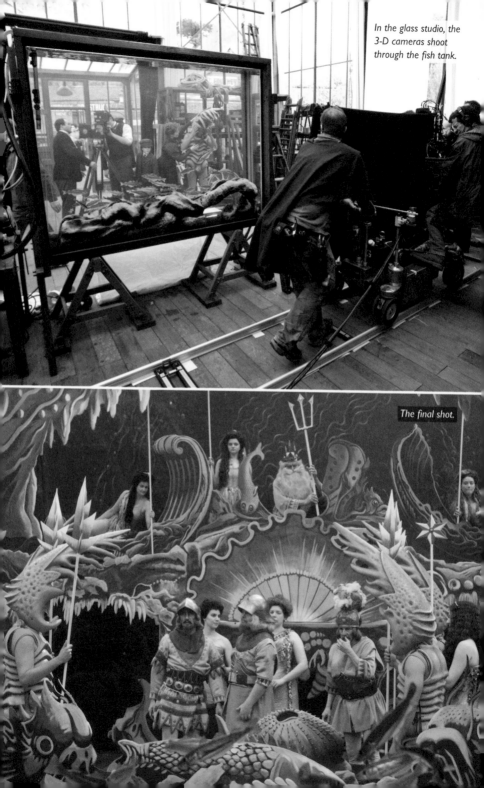

In the glass studio, the 3-D cameras shoot through the fish tank.

The final shot.

Hugo (Asa Butterfield) putting together a complicated mechanism.

CHAPTER THREE

ASSEMBLING
THE TEAM

Graham King

PRODUCER

Graham King says, "My job is to find a great story and then find the best people to make it come to life on screen. A producer is involved in every step of filmmaking, ensuring that his initial vision of the story stays intact while welcoming the ideas of everyone involved."

Graham grew up in North London, England, and has always loved movies. He says, "My producing partner Tim Headington and I were enchanted by Brian Selznick's book. Immediately we thought it would be a beautiful story for Martin Scorsese to create into a piece of cinema." Graham previously collaborated on three other pictures with Scorsese, and sent him the book for his directing consideration. Johnny Depp also joined the team as a producer, "and the rest is filmmaking history.

"Marty was perfect for this project since we needed someone with a specific visual style and a true passion for telling this story of Hugo's world. We also really wanted Hugo's environment to become as much a character as the actors, and 3-D is the ideal way to do that. All of Scorsese's films have a specific sensibility to them and *Hugo* is no different. The beautiful imagery and fantastic performances are all there. The main difference is that this film is not made solely for an adult audience — it is for everyone."

Graham King (right) and Martin Scorsese. Speaking of working together and adapting The Invention of Hugo Cabret, Graham says, "Marty and his team bring words and illustrations to life like no one else can. Their attention to detail has created such a magical world."

John Logan

John Logan explains that "the screenplay provides all the lines for the actors to speak, and it describes the action of the movie. I had to cut and change elements of Brian's book to make a more streamlined, shorter movie. The drawings were helpful because they reminded me of movie storyboards. They presented a road map for me to follow. For example, I opened the screenplay with a description very similar to Brian's first drawings in the book."

John remembers his childhood in California and New Jersey as being pretty normal and suburban, "except my parents are from Ireland so I was raised with a lot of poetry and books. I loved Sherlock Holmes and Jules Verne." When he was eight, John saw Laurence Olivier's movie version of *Hamlet*. "It led me toward Shakespeare, theater, and — inevitably — writing."

For John, the difference between writing a book and writing a screenplay comes down to the way a story is told. "In a movie, you *observe* the characters and learn about them through action, and what they say, not by going into their heads. We only know what Hugo is thinking in the movie by his words, by the expression on the actor's face, and by the way the director films it.

"I just wanted the screenplay to have the same emotional wallop that the book does."

1 INT. TRAIN STATION -- GRAND HALL - DAY   1

From far above it looks like a great clockwork.

We are looking down on the Grand Hall of the Paris Train Station.

It is crowded.

People bustle back and forth.

Like the gears and wheels of a clock.

A precise, beautiful machine.

We float down...

Under the great iron girders...

Moving through the station...

Past kiosks and shops...

Weaving among commuters...

Heading toward the trains and platforms in the distance...

Finally moving up to...

A huge clock suspended from the ceiling of the station...

Behind the ironwork dial we see a face peering out.

<u>HUGO CABRET</u> looks at us. He is a serious-looking boy of around 12. Long hair.

It is 1931.

2 INT. TRAIN STATION -- TUNNELS - DAY   2

Hugo turns away from the dial and moves through the tunnels behind the clock.

A serpentine maze of passageways.

Behind the walls.

Hugo's secret world.

<u>We move with him</u> as he goes quickly up and down spiral staircases ... ducking through tiny openings ... swerving in and out of dark passages ... up and down, back and forth...

Like an elaborate game of Chutes and Ladders.

He finally stops. Peers through another clock dial into a different part of the station.

                 (CONTINUED)

Hugo (Asa Butterfield) behind the clock, looking out at the train station in the opening of the movie.

Chris Surgent

FIRST ASSISTANT DIRECTOR

Chris Surgent describes his job as being "basically the director's right-hand man and his key link to the cast and the crew. Our collaboration on this movie began in pre-production after Marty had created a master plan of the story, going through each scene of the script and figuring out all of the shots he'd need to create his own unique vision. We both have our roles; his is the creative part and mine is the logistical part. He dreams it up and I help him get it on the screen."

Chris grew up on the New Jersey shore. "I enjoyed a pretty typical boyhood, playing Little League, making forts, and having summers on the beach. The first movie I remember seeing was *The Love Bug* when I was four years old. At thirteen, I watched Scorsese's *Taxi Driver*. It was a lot for me to handle so I had to shut it off whenever something violent happened. It took me about two weeks to watch the ending." Years later, Chris became a Directors Guild trainee and met Scorsese on the set of one of his movies.

"First thing I do on any film is break the script down into its individual scenes and determine what elements will be required from the various departments. For *Hugo*, this included anything ranging from Hugo's pocket watch (a prop) to Papa Georges's beard (makeup) to the train smashing through the station (special and visual effects) to three hundred background artists (costume, hair, and makeup).

"Scorsese concentrates on the performance of the actors and how all the various elements come together in a scene. I make sure the actors are prepared, that we have a quiet and focused working environment on set, that all the departments are prepared, and the various elements needed are available and ready.

"Any time you work on a project with Marty, it is an education. There are a lot of aspects of collaborating with him that are interesting and rewarding, but the lessons I learn about film history and our collective film heritage are my favorite. For example, while prepping *Hugo* we watched thirteen hours of Georges Méliès films, about 180 films in all. As part of our 3-D study, Marty screened *House of Wax* (1953) and *Dial 'M' for Murder* (1954). We screened the films of René Clair and Carol Reed, avant-garde cinema from the 1920s and '30s. We watched the Lumière Brothers' films and silent films from the 1920s to study period tinting and toning. We even studied the photography of Brassaï for the period look of the Parisian streets and the look and behavior of the background actors.

"Once shooting begins, the movie set can best be described as *controlled chaos*. My role, and the way I help Marty, is to control the chaos."

Chris Surgent (right) and Martin Scorsese with a member of the tech crew and Méliès's fire-breathing dragon, in the re-creation of the glass studio during a flashback scene. Because of the funny costumes and strange sets, these scenes were some of the most fun for the cast and crew to shoot.

Ellen Lewis

CASTING DIRECTOR

Ellen Lewis's job is to help Martin Scorsese find the perfect actor to play each role. "Growing up in Chicago, I was very affected by movies like *A Streetcar Named Desire* because of the realism and the emotional depth of the actors. Being a casting director is the perfect match for me, as I loved painting, but wasn't very good. I now get to be involved in painting a very big picture.

"To start casting, I have an early conversation with Marty about the tone he is looking for. I then put lists of names together. For Méliès, Marty knew very quickly that he wanted to go with Sir Ben Kingsley. Also, I know certain actors have come up over the years who Marty has been anxious to work with, like Sir Christopher Lee.

"When you are looking for kids, you cast as wide a net as possible." Ellen found Asa Butterfield, who plays Hugo, in London, while Chloë Moretz, who plays Isabelle, made a tape of herself reading for the part.

Ellen had just begun to think about the role of the Station Inspector when she got a call from someone representing Sacha Baron Cohen, who is best known for his wild comedic improvisations. "I took a long pause because I always try to imagine what that person would be. I just thought, 'What an interesting and different way to think of the role.' Marty immediately loved the idea."

Ben Kingsley

Asa Butterfield

Chloë Moretz

Sacha Baron Cohen

Sir Ben Kingsley

Georges Méliès

Sir Ben Kingsley grew up in the North of England, and has always felt a deep connection to the movies. "To this day, walking into a cinema is like walking into a church for me. I find cinemas very comforting and one of my *huge* childhood memories is being taken to see a movie when I was maybe five years old. The young star of the film was an Italian child, a character named Peppino, and I looked like the star's twin! I was completely emotionally swept away by the film, and at the end of the screening, the theater owner recognized that I was identical to the boy on the screen. He lifted me above the audience in the foyer. I was probably still sobbing and wiping tears, and he shouted, 'Little Peppino! Little Peppino!' Here I was, being held above the heads of the audience in this man's arms, being celebrated as the star of the movie. I thought, 'Well, this is pretty nice.' So I think that's when I became addicted to applause and stardom."

When Sir Ben was a teenager, he was the secretary of the Film Society in his school, where he became well versed in silent films, including those of Georges Méliès. "*A Trip to the Moon* was very much part of my wider imagination, a point of reference." So, in a way, Sir Ben was prepared when, nearly forty years later, Martin Scorsese phoned his house and said, "I am doing *Hugo*, and I'd like you to play Georges Méliès."

Speaking of the research he did for his work on the movie, Sir Ben says, "Of course I watched all of Georges's films, but it's not a question for me of preparation and research. That's minimal. It doesn't really teach you anything about what it's like to be Georges. But then, working with Marty, who is such a genius, I realized that my role model for playing Georges Méliès should be Martin Scorsese! There he is. Why look any further? You don't have to go out and research somebody who's been dead a long time whom you can't speak to. You are with a living pioneer of cinema, in the same room, day after day. It was like making cinema history about cinema history.

"At the toy booth, it was an absolute joy at first because I knew that I was the closest I would ever get to looking like an old photograph of Georges Méliès. It's a lovely feeling. It was a toy booth in a *vast* railway station. Everywhere I looked there were extras, trains, passengers, smoke, steam. It was an entire world. But for Georges, remembering his past would be too painful. So there was a kind of blackness to him in that toy booth. He's a sleepwalker, and nothing must wake him up. And of course, life *will* wake you up. And here's this wonderful little boy, who says, 'I'm here to drag you back into life!' It's classic mythology."

Drawing of Georges Méliès from
The Invention of Hugo Cabret.

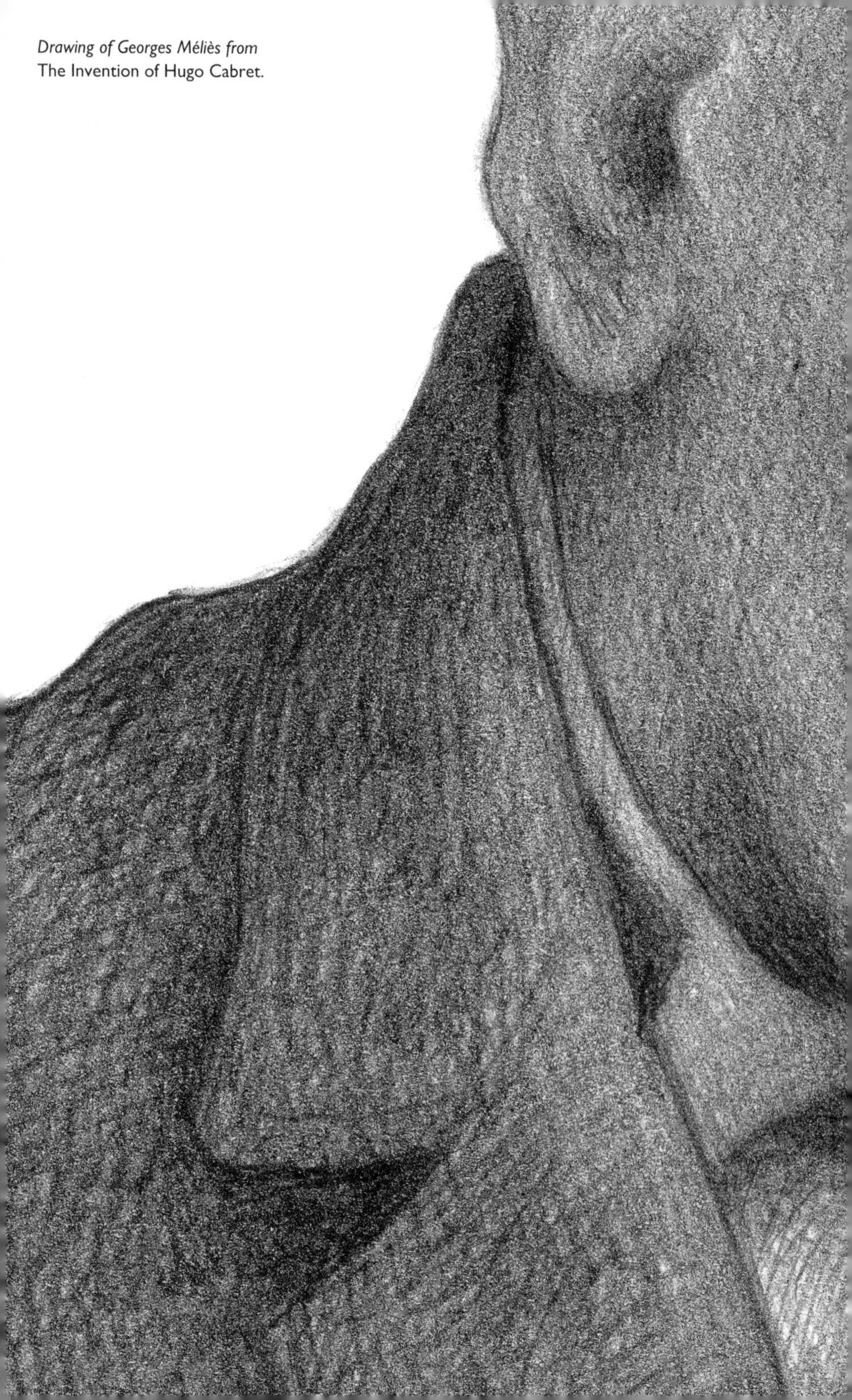

Ben Kingsley was aged and padded to look like Georges Méliès.

Georges Méliès (Ben Kingsley) watches in delight during the filming of one of his movies as spirals of smoke from a filmed explosion fall all around him.

Georges Méliès (Ben Kingsley) looking dapper on stage at his gala.

Georges Méliès (Ben Kingsley) burns his old props. This scene was filmed outdoors on a very cold night, but the fire was so hot that he almost burned his eyebrows.

GEORGES MÉLIÈS: MAGICIAN OF THE STAGE AND SCREEN

by David Serlin

Georges Méliès

Georges Méliès was born to a family of shoemakers in Paris in 1861. He rejected shoemaking to fulfill his dream of becoming a magician. Using money from the sale of the family shoe factory, he purchased a theater for magic that once had been owned by Jean-Eugène Robert-Houdin (the magician who inspired a young Ehrich Weiss to change his name to Harry Houdini).

When he was thirty-four, Méliès witnessed a brand-new invention — moving pictures — and realized right away the vast potential that this new art form held. Thinking about the magic tricks he created on stage at his theater, Méliès wondered what kind of tricks he could create using a camera. He soon began to build his own motion picture cameras and projectors, sometimes using spare parts from the automatons that Robert-Houdin had left behind in his former theater.

Many of Méliès's early films were attempts to re-create his stage performances. But as he began to master the camera, he also began to experiment with storytelling techniques, and created some of the first special effects (for instance, he discovered that by cutting the film in a certain way, he could make objects and people appear and disappear with ease). In 1902, he made what many people consider to be his masterpiece, the fourteen minute *Le voyage dans la lune* (*A Trip to the Moon*), and by 1914, he had made over five hundred films. He was a writer, director, actor, producer, and designer, and is considered by many to be the father of narrative film as well as science fiction films. Méliès's films encompassed everything from fairy tales to re-creations of recent news events. But by the time World War I erupted, audience tastes had changed and Méliès, with his unmoving camera, couldn't compete with directors who swept their cameras across great deserts and brought the viewer out into the action. Destitute, he was forced to sell copies of his films to a company that melted down the celluloid to make shoe heels, a tragic ending for the films of a man who had worked so hard to escape his parents' shoe factory. He abandoned his studio and burned the sets and costumes.

In the 1920s, Méliès began working seven days a week at a toy booth at the Gare Montparnasse, a train station in central Paris. He and his second wife Jehanne d'Alcy (whose real name was Fanny Manieux) raised his granddaughter after the girl's mother died and her father realized he couldn't take care of her on his own. Although Méliès felt defeated, it was during this period that a group of artists known as the Surrealists rediscovered his work (*surreal* is a French word meaning "outside of, or beyond the real world"). The Surrealists recognized an affinity between their work and the dreamlike worlds created by Méliès's films. Renewed interest in his career inspired a gala event in Paris where Méliès screened many of his old films. At the time of his death in 1938, he was back at work on a new film, *The Ghosts of the Metro*.

JOUETS

15.7-3

CONFISER

CHEMINS de FER de L'ÉTAT

LES ILES de L'OCÉAN
Église de St-Martin-de-Ré

*Georges Méliès (Ben Kingsley) in the toy booth,
re-created for the movie down to the last detail.*

Asa Butterfield

HUGO CABRET

Asa Butterfield was thirteen years old when he played Hugo. He lives in London, England, and has an older brother and a baby sister. "When I was about seven, my brother went to this acting club just for fun, and I started going to it. I never really thought of acting as anything other than something you do for fun. But one of the first auditions I got was *The Boy in the Striped Pajamas*." Asa was cast in the lead role and spent three months in Budapest filming it.

Three years later, Asa found out that he'd been cast in *Hugo* while he was at school. "Someone came in and said, 'Your mum's at reception.' She was standing in the entrance with my brother. She had the biggest grin on her face. She said, 'You got it!'"

Asa says that Martin Scorsese helped teach him all about the history of the cinema. "I actually saw the film which inspired Marty to become a director, *The Magic Box*." Asa also watched the silent movie *Safety Last*, starring Harold Lloyd, who at one point ends up hanging from the hands of a giant clock high over the city. Asa re-created that moment in *Hugo*. "I was in a big harness, which they attached to the ceiling so I wouldn't fall.

There was quite a drop below me."

To research his role, Asa says, "I did a lot with screw-drivers, making clocks. The props guy gave me a really nice set of tiny, fine screwdrivers. And I got one of those eyepieces. I was trying to get a watch face on, with screws that were literally less than a millimeter across. So I'd hold it quite up close with this little eyepiece magnifier, and I'd take it apart and put it back together again."

Like the clocks, Hugo's relationship with the automa-ton is a big part of the story. "I thought it was going to look like the Tin Man in *The Wizard of Oz*, with a tin head, a bit clunky. But when I saw it, it looked so human. It was like having another actor there. We named it Tom Tom."

There are scenes in the movie where Hugo is holding the automaton and weeping, and it's very clear that his connection with the machine is powerful. When asked about what was going through his mind during scenes like this, Asa replied, "A lot of actors say, 'When they start rolling the camera, I *become* whoever the character is.' But when I'm acting, I don't really feel like I become the character. I just think, *Okay, if I was Hugo, what would I be feeling right now? And what would I be doing? What would I be looking at? How would I be walking?* That sort of thing. And I just use that in my acting. I *imagine* what it would be like to be in his shoes."

Drawing of Hugo running from the Station Inspector in The Invention of Hugo Cabret.

Hugo (Asa Butterfield) runs through the café as he's chased by the Station Inspector. Chris Surgent would sometimes use a bullhorn to startle Asa during filming! The tracks you see on the ground are for the camera, and not for a train.

Hugo (Asa Butterfield) weeps as he desperately holds onto the automaton. When asked what it was like to hold the automaton, Asa said, "It was surprisingly heavy, but also very lifelike, almost like a child."

Asa Butterfield (Hugo) watches as Martin Scorsese demonstrates how the automaton is going to write. Asa says that when he auditioned for the movie, he had never heard of Scorsese, but people told him what a big deal it was, and now he's a huge fan of the director's work, especially The Aviator *and* The Departed.

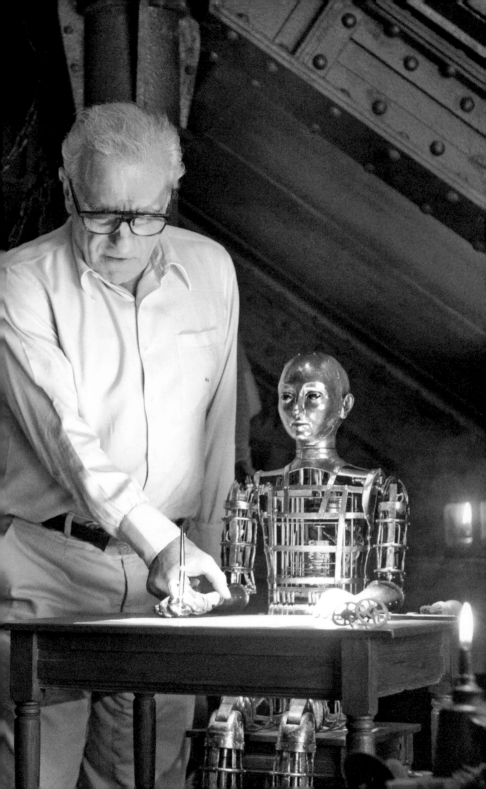

Asa Butterfield (Hugo) wears a harness as he dangles from the hand of the giant tower clock, re-creating a famous scene from Harold Lloyd's movie Safety Last. As the time changed, and the hand moved to the next number on the clock, it caused Asa to drop about two and a half feet each time. The harness was uncomfortable, but necessary. It was a long way down!

Chloë Moretz

ISABELLE

Chloë Moretz, like Asa, was thirteen years old when she played Isabelle. She was born in Atlanta, Georgia, and has four older brothers. "I first wanted to be an actor when I saw my brother preparing for his scene study classes while he was a musical theater student. I could not read fluently at that time, but I would memorize his scenes from listening to him rehearse them." Since then, Chloë and her family have moved to Los Angeles, where she has done lots of films. You might remember her from the movie version of Jeff Kinney's wonderful book *Diary of a Wimpy Kid*.

"Films set in the present are a bit easier to do because the trappings are commonplace and seen in everyday life. When doing a period piece, it requires research and a great imagination. For *Hugo*, since Asa and I did not live in the 1930s, we had to believably portray two children growing up in Paris under difficult circumstances. In the 1930s, you didn't have text messaging and stuff. So you actually had to go and talk to the person. And I think that's a cool part of it, because Hugo and Isabelle aren't running around with their cell phones looking up 'Georges Méliès.' They're having to figure it out through books and through studying. They're not always pulling out their phones and saying, 'Wait, I have a text!'

"Marty gave me a couple of Audrey Hepburn films to watch, *Roman Holiday* and *Funny Face*. I put a bit of Audrey in Isabelle.

"I love the fact that Isabelle is so well-read. Books are her life and her means of escape from a lonely childhood. I read *Wuthering Heights* when I was on this film and I also read *David Copperfield* just before we began shooting.

"My favorite scene in the film is when Hugo and Isabelle go into the clock and look out over Paris. They share a very special moment and it is a sweet scene. The scale of the set was ginormous! It was a real working clock with moving cogs, and we had to maneuver around them. Along with the clothing and the detail on set, there's not one thing that can break you out of your character. You won't be walking on the set and see a Coke can in the corner.

"With acting, you get into the character. To me, Isabelle is a living person. I wanted her to have a little short bob haircut and to wear a beret, just like the book. Isabelle's clothes are exactly as I envisioned them as well. She wears wool coats and sweaters that are a bit ill-fitting because her family doesn't have enough money to buy her new clothes as she grows. When I slipped into Isabelle's clothing and beret I just felt like her."

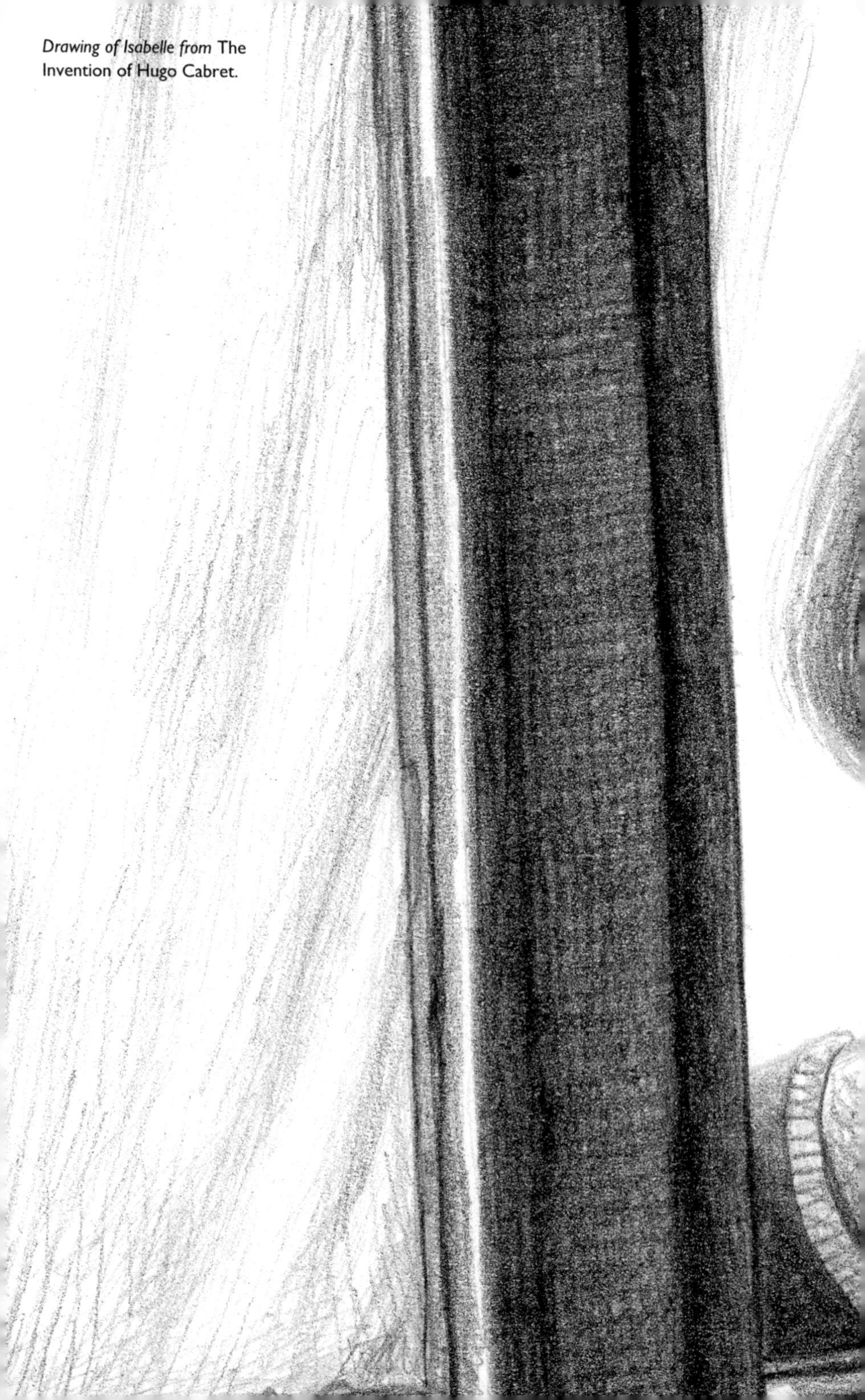

Drawing of Isabelle from The Invention of Hugo Cabret.

Isabelle (Chloë Moretz). By the end of filming Chloë had become an expert at flinging her beret up in the air and rolling it down one arm, behind her neck, down the other arm, and catching it.

Isabelle (Chloë Moretz) and Hugo (Asa Butterfield) in the hanging clock.

Chloë Moretz (Isabelle) and Asa Butterfield (Hugo) talk with Martin Scorsese outside the bookstore between shots. Chloë said that she was intimidated by the director when she first met him, but now she thinks of him as a "second dad."

Isabelle (Chloë Moretz) comforts Hugo (Asa Butterfield) in Hugo's secret apartment after he tries unsuccessfully to get the automaton to write.

Sacha Baron Cohen

THE STATION INSPECTOR

Unfortunately, Sacha Baron Cohen was unavailable to discuss his work on the movie, but Gustave Dasté, the Station Inspector himself, took a few minutes from his very busy schedule to talk with me.

"Sorry. I just had quite a long day. I am in charge of the discipline in the station. And I make sure that all the clocks are the right time, so I have a few watches. About two years ago, I found this clock that was almost eight minutes slow, and I reported the fact that it was slow to the man who winds the clocks. So that was *me* if you heard about that. I don't know if you heard about that in America.

"There's a lot of filthy, dirty children who tend to walk around the station and try and steal and pilfer things. And so I've taken it on myself to catch them and lock them up in a little cell and then send them off to the orphanage! There is an adolescent, quite an odious little character, quite a vicious little nasty little thing. He committed a terrible crime. . . . He stole a croissant. He stole it from Madame Emilie's café and so I've been trying to capture him. Not sure if the croissant can be returned fully uneaten because some of it may have been nibbled already. But I won't have that kind of disgusting filth happening in my station.

"In the war, I was in the trenches, World War I. Actually I don't call it World War I because it's the only one we've had. I just call it 'World War.' I accidentally shot myself. Since then I've had this little leg brace. It's hard to bathe with. And you must de-rust it quite well. I have a variety of screws and spanners. Oiling. Lathers, creams. It takes a lot of attention. It's quite squeaky.

"I was told by the authorities that we are making a documentary about the workings of the station, and it's being directed by this very loud American fellow. Ridiculous eyebrows . . . out of control eyebrows. I'm often going about my work and he's shouting, 'Cut!' and 'Action!' Scor-keys I think his name is. Marvin Scorkeys, he's an uncouth chap. No respect for the letter of the law, or for the etiquette in the station.

"He's brought with him a variety of different Americans, all of whom are shouting and making loud noises in the station. It's quite annoying. I don't see why it takes a hundred people to just light up a camera. I do not know what he's doing. Anyway, he ends up in the most peculiar places. The other day I was having a bath and next thing I knew this American director's in there — not *in* the bath — on the *outside* of the bath, filming it. I had the dog in the bath, scrubbing the dog, cleaning its underside. Next thing I know, this director is in the room with me asking if he could film!"

The Station Inspector (Sacha Baron Cohen)
in his office, bathing with his dog Maximilian.

Sir Christopher Lee

Monsieur Labisse, Bookseller

Sir Christopher Lee, who has made over two hundred and seventy movies, started his long, incomparable career at the age of six, playing Rumpelstiltskin in a school play in Switzerland. Soon he had moved to Britain and was performing Shakespeare at the age of eleven. Within a few years, he was sneaking onto the set of Laurence Olivier's *Hamlet*, to play a spear carrier. Now he has appeared in more movies than any other living actor, and says, "I've known Marty for thirty-five years. I told him that I didn't feel that my career was really ever complete until I'd done a film with him!

"What's it like to get ready to shoot? You go into makeup first. I didn't need much. Then you go into hairdressing. I was wearing a wig. And then you go to your dressing room. Wardrobe comes in, puts you in your clothes. And you start to try to read the newspaper, but you never succeed. You hear: 'All right, they're ready for you!' So I spent very little time in my dressing room, which is much nicer than spending a long time doing nothing. Marty knew what he wanted. The scene was set up, and we did maybe one, maybe two rehearsals. And then we were ready.

"All my scenes are with the kids. They're both extraordinary. No one's going to remember me!"

Monsieur Labisse (Christopher Lee) perched behind his desk. Christopher Lee always had amazing stories to share with everyone about his long career.

Richard Griffiths

MONSIEUR FRICK, NEWSPAPER VENDOR

Richard Griffiths grew up in Teesside, England, which was once famous for iron, steel, and coal. "My parents were both profoundly deaf and, therefore, mutely unable to speak. As a child, I had never heard a radio, and our first TV didn't arrive until I was thirteen. My earliest ambition was to become a painter, but I decided to study for a teaching qualification in English and drama. By the time I graduated, I had the intention of being a professional actor. I have earned my living as an actor ever since.

"Everyone's approach to acting has elements that are common, like knowing the lines, and remembering moves and actions that must be reproduced for continuity purposes. Development of character, movement, patterns of speech, emotional expression, and the type of intensity or energy required, all these are unique to each actor.

"In *Hugo*, my character, Monsieur Frick, had to be disliked and repeatedly challenged and threatened by Madame Emilie's dog. But the dog did not feel threatened enough to confront me. Consequently, he wouldn't snarl, growl, or bark when he was supposed to. Marty had to shoot all around the dogs to capture tiny movements of action we could use. You would think someone as energized as Marty would become impatient with the dogs' lack of cooperation. He didn't, but I did!"

Frances de la Tour

MADAME EMILIE, CAFÉ OWNER

Frances de la Tour was brought up in London. "My father was a documentary film director. My acting desires came from regularly going to the cinema as a child, almost obsessively. It was our one means of escape from an otherwise drab 1950s world just after the war. My elder brother, with me in tow, would dash through the bombed streets to see just about everything that was being shown in our local cinemas. Mainly we saw American films like *On the Waterfront*. I fell in love with the star of that movie, Marlon Brando. I wondered how I could act opposite him, and then I knew I had to become an actress first! I was ten, maybe eleven years old.

"In *Hugo*, the scenes with me and Richard Griffiths were shot like silent movies . . . that is to say our characters were seen from Hugo's point of view, mainly from afar. Marty mentioned Alfred Hitchcock's *Rear Window* from 1954. It is a film where a man in a wheelchair is observing actions in a faraway window. He sees two lovers at home. You can't hear the lovers, so their actions are exaggerated yet real nonetheless.

"Richard and I have worked together from as far back as twenty-five years ago, but we were required to act something we'd never done before. We had to be shyly in love with each other. Strangers in love!"

Monsieur Frick (Richard Griffiths) and Madame Emilie (Frances de la Tour) at a café table in the train station with the dogs that keep them apart and, finally, bring them together.

Helen McCrory

MAMA JEANNE

Helen McCrory grew up all over the world. "I was a toddler in Norway, a child in west and east Africa, and a teenager in Paris. My heroes were artists like Bob Dylan, Caravaggio, and Emile Zola. I think moving about taught me not to worry about what anyone else was doing.

"I knew I wanted to be an actress at school. Getting a good training, though, was tough. I'd set my heart on a school that at first rejected me. You have to be hard-working and patient to become what you want to be; it's no different now.

"In *Hugo*, playing a character at very different ages was fascinating. As an actress in her teens, my character was Jehanne d'Alcy, not Mama Jeanne. She was a muse to one of the greatest pioneers of filmmaking. She helped run the first film studio. A World War later, she had experienced the occupation of her city, the collapse of their studio, and her husband's breakdown. She was the same character, but time and circumstance rendered Jehanne d'Alcy and Mama Jeanne almost unconnected, until of course Hugo brings her husband, and therefore herself, contentment once again. It's Jehanne d'Alcy dancing with her husband in the last scene. It was wonderful for my character to be offered an opportunity to see herself as a young, happy, carefree movie star again."

Mama Jeanne (Helen McCrory) watches from the audience as her husband, Georges Méliès, is celebrated during the gala in his honor.

René Tabard (Michael Stuhlbarg) at the gala celebrating Georges Méliès, which was filmed at the Sorbonne, in Paris. The names of French philosophers and playwrights were chiseled into the walls amid beautiful paintings. Michael said it was as if the room was filled with ghosts!

Michael Stuhlbarg

RENÉ TABARD, PRESIDENT OF THE FRENCH FILM ACADEMY

Michael Stuhlbarg was born and raised in Long Beach, California. "I was a pretty self-sufficient, easygoing kid. I loved to draw and had wanted to be a cartoonist or an architect. The movies I remember loving were those of Bob Fosse, Stanley Kubrick, and Martin Scorsese. They captivated my imagination, and they each had such a unique visual vocabulary. You could immediately tell their films apart from all the others. They must have had an influence on my wanting to become an actor. I acted in my first play at the age of eleven. My love of art found its way into my profession. . . . I often sketch the characters I play to sort through all the possibilities of what they could look like."

As Michael prepared to play Tabard, he says, "Marty and I talked about the history of French cinema, particularly of Henri Langlois, cofounder of the Cinémathèque Française, and his passion for saving films. Marty talked of the seriousness with which films are taken in France. Since Tabard is an author, historian, and preservationist, I tried to see as many of the films made before 1931 as I could." Michael based Tabard's looks on a period photo he found of "a middle-aged intellectual. And noting how Tabard's preservationist passions mirrored Marty's, I grew out my eyebrows as a tribute to him."

Emily Mortimer

Lisette, the Flower Girl

Emily Mortimer was raised in an artistic household in London, England. "I was surrounded by books and fascinating people, but my response was just to watch endless amounts of terrible television. It was an amazing education. I saw every black-and-white movie. I would go and sunbathe by the swimming pool with a parasol, a blonde wig, and a bikini and try to be like a 1950s film star."

As the Station Inspector's love interest, Emily found herself doing a kissing scene . . . with the dog! "The trainer said, 'I'm going to put some sardine oil on your face. The dog will just give you a little kiss,' and I thought, *Oh, that's sweet.* Then suddenly, I'm face-to-face with this enormous Doberman pinscher who has been commanded to lick me all over my face. It was really weird."

Emily was cast in *Hugo* very soon after having a baby. Happily married with children, she found it hard at first to imagine what Lisette's life would have been like. "She's a lonely lady, but her whole job is about making other people happy with flowers. Because of World War I, everybody felt vulnerable and alone. Lisette and the Inspector have coped with it in opposite ways. He's become this slightly twisted, angry person, and she's become a bright, clean person. It's just two sides of the same coin, I suppose."

Lisette (Emily Mortimer) at the flower booth where she makes her living and pines for the Station Inspector.

Uncle Claude (Ray Winstone) has another drink in the secret apartment.

Ray Winstone

UNCLE CLAUDE

Ray Winstone was born in the East End of London, in a section of town called Hackney. "I started boxing at about the age of thirteen," Ray says. "Most of the kids I grew up with went boxing." But Ray did better than most. He was three times London Schoolboy Champion. Ray also loved the movies as a kid. "My dad used to pick me up from school and take me to the cinema every Wednesday afternoon. It was a lot of war films because it wasn't too far after the Second World War."

Ray began acting when he was in school. His first play was *Emil and the Detectives*. "I played the newspaper boy. I must have been about eleven or twelve." Ray's childhood love of movies and acting, as well as the toughness he displayed as a boxer have all combined for the part he plays in *Hugo*, Uncle Claude, a character who spends much of his time drunk. "You've got to try to walk straight, basically. You try not to overdo it. I mean, there's comedy drunk, and there's drunk-drunk, so I was kind of, like, pickled, you know?

"But the joy for me during filming was actually watching Scorsese work, because it was like he was falling in love with making a film again. Watching him with 3-D, with something he'd never worked with before . . . it was like watching a kid with a new toy."

Jude Law

HUGO'S FATHER

Jude Law grew up in London and was a huge Charlie Chaplin fan when he was a little boy. "My dad used to have reels of Chaplin films he projected at our birthday parties. *The Circus* was my particular favorite, and I loved *City Lights*." That movie was released in 1931, the year that *Hugo* takes place.

"I knew the book because I'd already read it to my children. So I went back and reread it, and I talked to my children about it and asked them their impressions of the father. The glasses were a little detail that I was very keen on keeping because I remembered him wearing glasses in the book. I got to talk to a clockmaker, and I looked at automatons, so I had a certain knowledge of how to hold things, and if they were referring to tools, I'd know what they were. But otherwise, to me, really, it was simply about creating a very warm and heartfelt chapter to Hugo's life, knowing that the majority of the story sets him in quite a cold world. I wanted to make sure that you realize he had been loved. I thought it was really important that I carry my experiences of being a father into it.

"Working with Asa was just a joy, and I think it was a relief to him to have a week where he could be *happy*, without feeling like he was being chased, or terrorized by someone!"

Hugo's father (Jude Law) cares for the automaton, which he rescued from a burning museum.

Cameos

A *cameo* is when someone makes an unexpected and brief appearance in a movie. There are several cameos in *Hugo*. Martin Scorsese's daughter Francesca appears with Chris Surgent's daughter Emily in the tea dance in the café, and Graham King's daughter Samantha appears in the party scene at the end of the movie. The actor Michael Pitt can be seen briefly as a projectionist, and Sir Ben Kingsley's son Edmund appears as well, as a cameraman. Finally, Martin Scorsese himself has a cameo, as the photographer in the flashback sequence. See if you can spot everyone when you watch the movie.

*Francesca Scorsese (left)
and Emily Surgent*

Samantha King

Michael Pitt

Edmund Kingsley

Martin Scorsese

Dante Ferretti's Parisian graveyard, built at Shepperton Studios in England. The sculpted tombs were inspired by funerary figures Martin Scorsese had seen at the Metropolitan Museum of Art in New York City.

CHAPTER FOUR

LIGHTS!
CAMERA!
DESIGN!

Dante Ferretti

PRODUCTION DESIGNER

Dante Ferretti was responsible for the massive sets on which Martin Scorsese filmed *Hugo*. This movie marks the first time in his fifty-year career that Dante has worked on an adaptation of a book with illustrations. "When I saw the pictures in *The Invention of Hugo Cabret*, it was most helpful."

Dante and his team created from scratch a life-size train station, Méliès's entire apartment building, a bombed-out structure next door, a fully stocked wine shop on the corner, an enormous graveyard filled with huge monuments and stone crypts made out of fiberglass following Dante's designs, and much more.

Growing up in Macerata, Italy, Dante says, "I was in the fine arts school when I was twelve, and every afternoon I went to see movies. It was a small town, but there were six movie theaters, so I grew up inside the movie theater! There was *Ben-Hur*, there was *Cleopatra*. Also, I liked many Westerns. I thought, *Oh, I want to work in this business.*"

Dante's best friend when he was eight or nine was a boy whose father worked with clocks. "There was a big clock tower in the main square and every day the father and son would wind the clock. Many times I would help them. Sometimes the father was sick, and my friend and

I went alone to wind it. When Martin told me about the book *The Invention of Hugo Cabret,* I thought, *Oh, my God, look at this! I know this very well!* And all my memory about this came back. Before working on this movie I'd forgotten everything."

Dante, along with the rest of the crew and the cast, spent two weeks in Paris, filming in two theaters, a giant library, and on a few streets that they transformed with signs, posters, fake snow, vintage cars, and new shopwindows. Everything else was built in England. "We made everything so big and perfect like a Paris postcard.

"Marianne Bower gave us a lot of research. And then we pulled all the stuff together to make a mosaic with everything, also with little bits of fantasy. That's important. What I always try to do when I do this job is not copy, but try to be like an occupant of the time period so I can put something of myself inside. We liked doing the train station very much, and all the tunnels! It was like being inside a brain. You go from inside the ear and you walk inside the brain, and then come out the other side. Hugo is behind the clock, like he is behind the eye, and he looks at what happens outside!"

Dante was also very inspired by the old movies that Scorsese had everyone watch. For instance, he made the staircase leading up to the Méliès apartment just like the one in Truffaut's *The 400 Blows*. "We're making stories that are about the history of movies, so it makes sense to be inspired by the movies that came before us."

This full-size French train station was built from scratch on a soundstage in Shepperton Studios in England.

Hugo runs through the train station in a drawing from The Invention of Hugo Cabret.

Model of train station, built by Dante's team. Dante says, "Because the model is already in 3-D, Marty can see everything and know exactly where he'll have to put the camera."

B STAGE INT AREA : 36.57M X 30.48M X 10.78M (HEIGHT)   A STAGE INT AREA : 45.72M X 36.58M X 12.07M (HEIGHT)

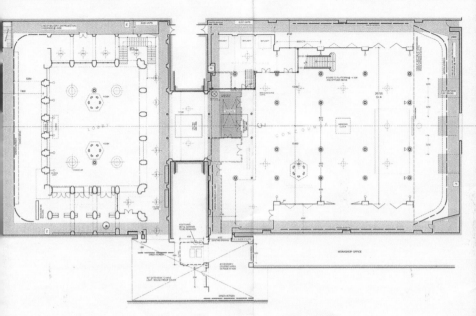

Floor plans of the entire train station. This set, when built, was approximately one hundred and fifty feet long by one hundred and nineteen feet wide by forty-one feet high.

Hugo amid the crowd in a drawing from The Invention of Hugo Cabret.

Hugo behind the walls of the train station in a drawing from The Invention of Hugo Cabret.

Asa Butterfield (Hugo) being filmed behind the walls of the train station.

Hugo (Asa Butterfield) and Isabelle (Chloë Moretz) outside the movie theater in Paris. The snow is made out of Epsom salts.

Hugo walking down a street in Paris in a drawing from The Invention of Hugo Cabret.

Dante Ferretti's drawing of Hugo's secret apartment.

Hugo (Asa Butterfield) alone in his secret apartment. For much of the shoot, Asa and the first assistant director, Chris Surgent, had an ongoing game of rock, paper, scissors.

Hugo in his secret apartment in a drawing from The Invention of Hugo Cabret.

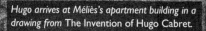
Hugo arrives at Méliès's apartment building in a drawing from The Invention of Hugo Cabret.

Hugo (Asa Butterfield) arrives at Méliès's apartment building.

Francesca Lo Schiavo

SET DECORATOR

Francesca Lo Schiavo's job was to create the atmosphere on the set with furniture and all the decorative little details that bring the world of *Hugo* to life. Among other things, she chose all the clocks and watches in Hugo's father's apartment until it was bursting with gold and brass, and she stocked the café with period china and silverware. She placed letters on the mantelpiece in the Mélièses' bedroom and filled Hugo's secret apartment with jars of mechanical parts. "When I began my work on *Hugo*, Martin said to me that what I do should resonate with what Brian did. For example, in the bookstore, I tried to get all the details of the art in a large scale. We found a lot of books, forty thousand or fifty thousand. So it was huge, but at the same time, I tried not to lose the fact that it was a secret hiding place for the kids."

Francesca, like her husband Dante Ferretti, is from Italy. "I grew up in Rome. I loved to go to the movies when I was a kid, but my parents didn't allow me to go very often. It was the most wonderful treat. I would be in heaven." Francesca always enjoyed art, and eventually became an interior decorator. Then she met Dante, who invited her to see a set for a film he was designing. "So I went to visit. Dante said to me, 'Why don't you try to do this job in films?'

"I did a lot of drawings for this film, for the scale, for the proportions. All the lighting was made from scratch." She also did a huge amount of shopping. "Ah, the shopping! The shopping was in flea markets in Paris. I went to a French prop house as well, and found some French china. The tables and the chairs came from Paris, even the cutlery, to create the right atmosphere. Not only the big things . . . because Martin asked me to go for magic. So we made a lot of the toys in the toy booth.

"Martin wanted to do a lot with the posters in the station, too. The posters were one of the heroes of the film for him. In the 1930s, there were plenty of posters, so Martin and Marianne chose carefully and I helped, to make them in the right style."

All the posters throughout the movie comment on the story of Hugo's life and adventures. You'll see posters that feature pictures of eyes, and shoes, and ones that advertise important movies from the time period. Above the flower booth in the train station is a gigantic magazine poster, almost the size of a movie screen, with an image of a mysterious figure lying across it. A single eye in an abstract profile is staring directly at its heart, and if you look very carefully, you'll notice that the heart is shaped just like the keyhole on the automaton!

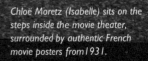
Chloë Moretz (Isabelle) sits on the steps inside the movie theater, surrounded by authentic French movie posters from 1931.

Lisette's flower booth bursts with color beneath the giant poster with the figure that evokes the automaton.

The tea dance at the café. Martin Scorsese thought the hired dancers looked too professional, so extras were taught to dance at the last minute.

Isabelle in the bookstore in a drawing from The Invention of Hugo Cabret.

The bookstore in the train station, with over 40,000 books towering up to the ceiling.

The clocks in Hugo's father's apartment.

Hugo's father works on the clocks in a drawing from The Invention of Hugo Cabret.

David Balfour

David Balfour was in charge of the team that created the props in the movie, including the automaton. David works on the props that the cast interacts with, like Hugo's father's notebook, and the skittering mechanical mouse in the toy booth. In the prop warehouse, every surface was covered with objects to be used for the movie. There were thousands of books, hundreds of suitcases, rows of walking sticks, clock parts, magic tricks, posters, furniture, toys, and vintage cameras for as far as the eye could see. "All the props were well researched. Scorsese would always be keen to know how they worked, so everything had to be made as accurately as possible, sometimes using modern technology to make pieces work as they would have when first built."

David grew up in Glasgow, Scotland, and says, "The person who probably had the most influence on me and who helped shape my career was my brother, Ross. He was a carpenter. He worked in the shipyards and then made his way into the theater, where he became a master carpenter. I was a bit wayward and he took me in, got me a job in the theater workshop, and changed my life. He moved on to film, I followed, and here I am. Without him, I would not be the person I am today."

As David worked on the props for *Hugo*, he says, "I referenced the original book constantly, in fact I made up my own book with just the illustrations and used that as inspiration. It is a huge part of my job to get things right.

"The development and design of the automaton was a long process and after studying original automatons, we had to create our version. I wanted to give it a personality but not too different from the image in the book. Scorsese was very precise in what he wanted and the size was crucial. It was also very important that a relationship could develop between Hugo and the automaton, and the best way for that to happen for me was in its expression. The problem in the beginning was that it looked too mechanical and a little alien. In trying to tell its own story of being abandoned and then brought back to life by Hugo and his father, we thought it would be good to subtly change its expression from sad to happy when it is finally restored."

In the end, David Balfour and his team created fifteen different automatons, each built for a different function in the movie, with expressions that transform as the story progresses. "The *Mona Lisa* became an inspiration after much discussion with Scorsese. It seemed obvious that the much debated and enigmatic expression of the painting could be the look that we were after. You are never quite sure what the automaton is thinking!"

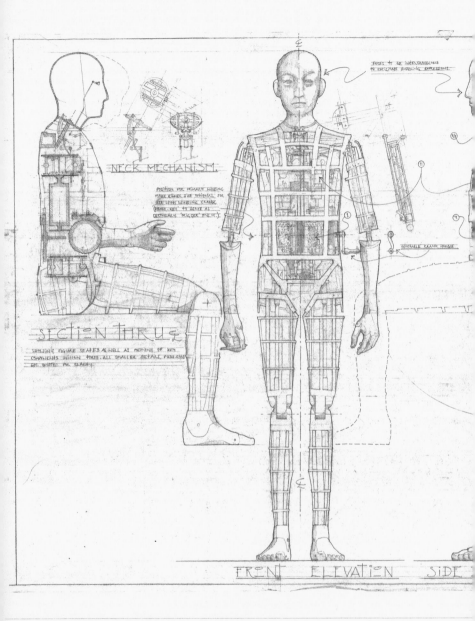

NECK MECHANISM.

POSITION FOR PRIMARY WINDING MADE EITHER SIDE OPTIONAL FOR USE WITH WINDING CRANK. (REAR KEY TO SERVE AS SECONDARY 'BIGGER' JOINT.)

SECTION THRU.

SHOWING FIGURE SEATED AS WELL AS MOTIONS OF KEY CHANGES WITHIN TORSO. ALL SMALLER DETAILS OMITTED RE: SHOWN RE: CLARITY.

FACES TO BE INTERCHANGEABLE TO FACILITATE DIFFERING EXPRESSIONS.

REMOVABLE COLLAR TONGUE

FRONT ELEVATION   SIDE

Blueprint for the automaton, showing all the mechanisms and movements of the complicated parts.

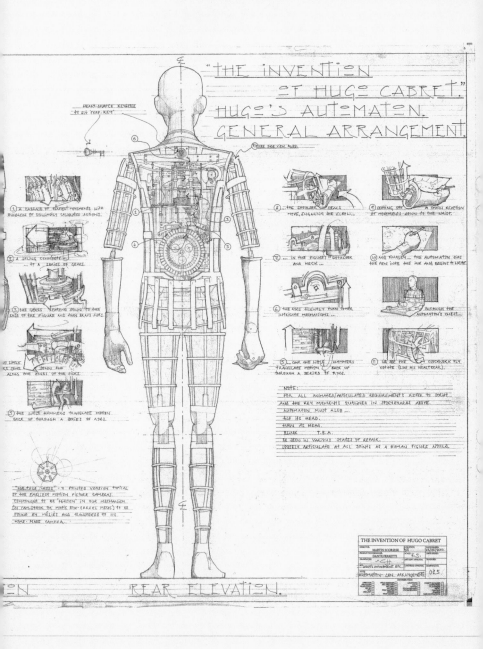

"THE INVENTION
OF HUGO CABRET."
HUGO'S AUTOMATON.
GENERAL ARRANGEMENT.

REAR ELEVATION.

The Mona Lisa by Leonardo da Vinci in the Louvre Museum. Notice her enigmatic smile.

One of the fifteen different automatons built for the movie. This one is just beginning to smile.

Asa Butterfield (Hugo) in the hanging clock. In the foreground you can see the bucket of tools Hugo uses to fix the clocks. It was incredibly heavy, so for scenes where Asa had to carry it for a long time, the props department made an extra set of tools from hard rubber that look exactly the same, but weigh almost nothing.

A BRIEF HISTORY OF AUTOMATONS

by David Serlin

Vichy acrobat, 1870

The word *automaton* derives from the Greek, meaning "an object that can move by itself," and is related to the words *autonomous*, *automatic*, and *automobile*. Throughout history, automatons have referred to any number of mechanical objects, from wind-up animals in music boxes and wall clocks to full-scale animated figures and robots that are designed to simulate lifelike animal or human movement. In Greek mythology, for instance, Hephaestus, the god of blacksmithing and metallurgy, built a man out of metal and gave him human characteristics. In Jewish folklore, there is reference to a *golem*, an automaton made of mud or dust or other organic material that is animated into the shape of a man.

The quest to make autonomous life became easier with the invention of clocks during the Middle Ages. Clockmakers realized that the intricate cogs and wheels used to keep time could also be used to reproduce and mimic the actions of living organisms. During the thirteenth century, for example, the Arabic mathematician Al-Jazari built an elaborate automaton known as the Elephant Clock, which ran by itself. The most successful automatons were those that were the most lifelike. In 1739, the French inventor Jacques de Vaucanson created a sensation when he invented a mechanical duck that could flap its wings, drink water, eat food, and even relieve itself.

Magicians and showmen seized on the idea to incorporate automatons and other mechanical figures into their performances, and audiences were often unable to discern whether or not the figures were actually alive, which caused great excitement among the crowds. Soon magicians, along with entertainers, carnival sideshows, and even museums, were exhibiting mechanical figures that could walk a tightrope, play piano, perform magic tricks, shoot tiny arrows, and, like the automatons built by Henri Maillardet around 1800, write poems and draw pictures. In the nineteenth century, the French magician Jean-Eugène Robert-Houdin famously created an automaton named Antonio Diavolo, who swung on a trapeze, and to the shock of those who were sure it was wired through its arms, let go and hung by its knees. Many years later, Robert-Houdin's automatons were inherited by the filmmaker Georges Méliès.

There are still societies today composed of inventors, historians, artists, and engineers that are dedicated to the creation of new automatons and the maintenance of old ones. With the invention of computers and microelectronics, though, the idea of building an automaton may seem easier than ever, especially in the era of robots that can clean floors, play chess, and appear on game shows. But the "perfect" automaton, whose movements are indistinguishable from that of the human, remains a dream as elusive as the slippery hands of Antonio Diavolo.

Antonio Diavolo sitting on his trapeze, ready to amaze audiences.

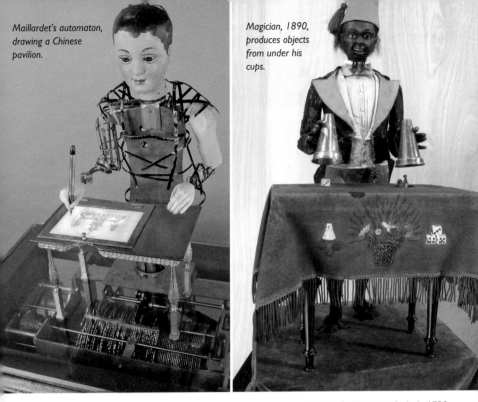

Maillardet's automaton, drawing a Chinese pavilion.

Magician, 1890, produces objects from under his cups.

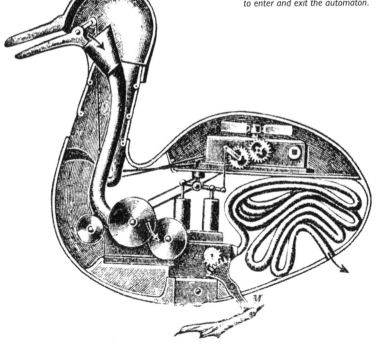

Diagram for Vaucanson's duck, 1739. You can see where the food is supposed to enter and exit the automaton.

Sandy Powell

Costume Designer

Sandy Powell designed all the clothing worn by the actors in *Hugo*. "When I started work on the movie I had a meeting with Marty and we discussed the fact that because it's a children's story, the principal characters shouldn't have lots of costume changes. Since there were hundreds of people in the background, and we'd be seeing everybody through Hugo's eyes, his point of view, the characters have to be instantly recognizable. So basically what I did was give each character a signature look and stuck to that. I wanted it to be very graphic."

Sandy grew up in London and says, "I've been aware of and interested in clothing as far back as I can remember. My mother made clothes for me and my sister, and I would help choose the colors and fabrics and patterns. The first clothes I made were for my dolls. I loved the spectacle of films as a child and always enjoyed fashion, but it never occurred to me that it could be a career until I was around thirteen or fourteen, when I saw films such as *Death in Venice* and *Cabaret*, and realized this was a world I wanted to be part of."

For *Hugo,* Sandy says, "I started each costume by meeting with the actor and trying on various outfits in order to discover what works the best in terms of shape, silhouette, color, and general summing up of the character. I then looked for fabrics and textures that I liked, and combined those with the successful items of clothing fitted to create the final costume."

In one flashback scene, the character of Mama Jeanne, as a young woman, levitates onstage in a spectacular dress. "I found part of the skirt in a flea market in Paris. That skirt must have been an old costume or an old fancy dress. It was from the 1940s or '50s. And then I built the rest of the dress.

"The Station Inspector's costume was really important. In the script it said he was wearing bottle green, but it just didn't feel right to me. I ended up with a strange color, sort of a turquoise. It's really not an obvious uniform color.

"In the case of Hugo, I put a sweater on him that I found. It was really falling apart but it just works because of the simplicity of those two stripes. Now, to me, that's just Hugo, that striped sweater." Sandy and her team needed several versions of the same outfit. "And we needed to make far more duplicates of both kids' clothes to allow for growth over the course of the shoot!

"For Méliès, I went by the photographs of the real person. At first I made the clothes and they looked like they were right, but it all looked wrong when it was first put on Sir Ben Kingsley. I finally realized it's because he was standing upright. I realized if we gave him padding it would remind him that he has to be more stooped and look a bit sadder."

Sandy Powell's costume sketches, alongside those same costumes she and her team made for the movie.

Station Inspector

Isabelle

Hugo Cabret

Georges

Jan Archibald

HAIR DESIGNER

Jan Archibald was responsible for designing all the hairstyles in the movie, from the stars of the film to the hundreds of extras. "I created different types of wigs for this production, many for the crowds in the railway station. Short hairstyles were the fashion in Paris in the 1930s, so I had to supply wigs for ladies and girls who had long hair and did not want to cut it."

Jan became interested in hair when she was a student and got a job working in an opera house in London, near where she grew up. "I was fascinated by the period styles and dressing techniques, as well as by the history. So researching the hair for *Hugo* was exciting." Along with the old movies everyone watched, she spent a long time looking at photographs of people in Paris in the 1930s, especially children.

"I had to communicate with my team of barbers, hair-dressers, and wig-dressers, and had long discussions about the best way to get everyone ready for the shoot in the mornings. We had three hundred wigs for this movie, plus some hairpieces for the scenes in the 1880s to 1900. To keep the cast's hair looking tidy, we had Eric the barber and his team cutting them every twelve to fourteen days. We did so many haircuts during the course of the shoot, possibly thousands."

Morag Ross

MAKEUP DESIGNER

Morag Ross conceived of the makeup to help the actors look glamorous, old, sad, or even dirty. She says, "Makeup for a movie has to maintain its effect of improving the skin tone color under strong film lighting. I designed a palette of period colors, including duck egg blue, burgundy brown, coral, and rose, all on a lovely pale ivory complexion. Makeup artists are on set at all times to do touch-ups and repairs after lunch or during scenes where crying is involved. Along with hairdressing and costume, makeup creates the visual characters for the story. I had a fantastic team of makeup artists who worked with me. It would be impossible to do all the work on a movie alone."

Morag grew up in Glasgow, Scotland. She never imagined that she would grow up to be a makeup artist for movies. But in her final year of high school, a teacher encouraged her to apply for a place at art college and "that, in my mind, is where my training as a makeup artist began."

On the set of *Hugo*, Morag and her team started each day very early, "maybe at six A.M., and we finished around seven P.M. Once basic filming is done for the day, we make sure that everyone has their makeup removed and their false mustaches cleaned and prepared for the next day's filming."

Ben Kingsley (Georges Méliès) watches as Morag Ross applies makeup to Helen McCrory (Mama Jeanne) as she prepares to film a flashback scene inside Méliès's glass studio.

Wigs and makeup created for the flashback scenes. Note the color charts and drawings.

The tent where all the extras got into costume, makeup, and hair. There were up to 500 extras on days when filming took place inside the train station.

Jan Archibald checks Helen McCrory's wig as she prepares to film a scene. Besides looking just right, everything had to be fireproof because this scene involved sparklers and fireworks and all sorts of explosives.

Robert Richardson

CINEMATOGRAPHER

Robert Richardson created the lighting for *Hugo* and also operated the main camera. He is the director of photography for the film, and works with a large team of assistants who, among other responsibilities, take care of the delicate cameras. Bob worked with brand-new 3-D cameras that represent the very latest in 3-D and digital technology. "My hope was to evoke a period, the 1930s in Paris, and yet not to divorce the present."

Bob grew up in Hyannis, Massachusetts, and seems to have always had an affinity for light. "I was born to Cape light. Fall and winter light have given me the greatest pleasure. The dust-like first snow, skeletal trees, dark, deep hues of violet-black. Films were a constant delight when I was young; in particular I loved *The Wizard of Oz*." Bob did not start working with cameras until he was in his early teens, but they quickly became an obsession.

Regarding the process of making movies, Bob says, "There is no smooth path. *Hugo* was a tremendous opportunity. The 3-D process was new and as such provided a stunning challenge, like building a castle in the air."

And speaking of air, when I first visited the set and watched the monitor as a scene was being filmed, I noticed glowing particles of dust shimmering through the air, which leapt out of the 3-D screen. It looked magical. I thought at first it was just luck that the lights Bob had set up happened to catch the dust in the air at the time of the shooting. I later learned that the dust was Bob's idea. He wanted viewers to really *feel* the atmosphere of the station. To create the dust, they experimented with different goose-down feathers, which were grated and blown into the air for each shot. Bob says, "I thought that soot and dust would help define or highlight the space . . . and space, or volume, is inherent to 3-D. Smoke was further used, as was dry ice."

The night Bob filmed Georges Méliès burning his old props outside his great glass studio, the moon was out, but the light wasn't bright enough for filming. A gigantic metal grid was built, filled with lightbulbs, covered in blue cloth, and then hoisted high into the sky by a giant crane. Suddenly the blue fabric lit up, and the night was awash in the most perfect and ethereal moonlight. Méliès began his bonfire, and Bob, riding his camera rig like it was a wild animal, swooped in over the flames, which licked toward the screen in 3-D.

"3-D enhances the viewing experience," he says. "It creates both an emotional and a physical presence. There is another shot within the film where the sun enters a voluminous library. Atmosphere was added with a white smoke so we could see the rays of light. In the film, they looked like they were solid beams of platinum. In my experience this could only be achieved by 3-D."

Robert Richardson riding a giant crane with the 3-D cameras on the streets of Paris, as bemused Parisians look out their windows to see what is going on.

Robert Richardson on the camera rig in the Bibliothèque Sainte-
Geneviève. Bob had prepared cranes outside the windows with
giant lights to simulate the sun, but when it was time to film,
the sun came cascading into the library, one window at a time.

Uncle Claude (Ray Winstone) comes to tell Hugo (Asa Butterfield) that his father has died in a fire. Robert Richardson's evocative lighting in this scene reflects the moods of the actors.

Larry McConkey

Larry McConkey explains that a Steadicam "is a device used to carry a camera in your hands while still being able to move it smoothly. There is a lot of film equipment to carry: the camera, the lens motors and radio, the monitor, and batteries to run it all. The Steadicam attaches to a strong vest or harness that clamps around your body. It has a mechanical arm with hinges and springs that lets it move around right under one of your own arms. The hard part is controlling it. It takes years of practice to do it well, a lot like the training needed to become a professional dancer."

Larry grew up in Ithaca, New York. "I have always loved books and music but also science and gadgets of all kinds. On *Hugo*, most of the time, Robert Richardson rode on a crane with the camera attached to the top. The camera glided around the actors and soared through the air. But sometimes we just couldn't get these large pieces of equipment where we wanted the camera to go. That's when I was asked to help. The extra challenge on this movie was to carry two cameras and lenses instead of just one on my Steadicam, because that is how to shoot the best-quality 3-D. For that reason, I wanted to use the same cameras that were being used on the cranes, and they were *heavy*, more than one hundred pounds!"

Larry McConkey, wearing the elaborate Steadicam device, stands on a platform that will soon lower to the ground so he can step off and continue filming.

Demetri Portelli

3-D STEREOGRAPHER

Stereography is the art of using two cameras to photograph the world in three dimensions, and Demetri Portelli explains that "it's just like the way the human brain uses two eyes in our head to see our surroundings and discern depth in space in front of us."

Demetri grew up in the suburbs outside of Toronto, Canada, and has been involved with cameras, either in front of them or behind them, since he was a kid. "I flirted with the idea of being an actor on and off for many years until I saw the first Indiana Jones movie. Then I went home and told my mom I wanted to make movies."

During the filming of *Hugo*, Demetri sat in front of a monitor wearing his 3-D glasses, holding a remote-control device. It looked a little like he was playing a video game, but he was controlling the two lenses on the 3-D camera as it was filming a scene. This is called *live 3-D* (as opposed to 3-D that is added later in a special effects studio). As the lenses moved, Demetri could manipulate how much depth the scene seems to have. "A good 3-D film should make you feel like you are looking right into someone's kitchen window. The objects should seem as if you could reach out and touch them. Like any good film, the images should captivate and enthrall you."

Demetri Portelli with one of the 3-D cameras. Demetri says, "I think of the 3-D rig now as a high-performance racing car. It takes a highly organized camera team of operators, camera assistants, technicians, and many others to manipulate the rig quickly and efficiently, like a pit crew at an auto race."

Rob Legato

Rob Legato had two important jobs on *Hugo*. As the second unit director, he helped Scorsese attain some of the shots that were necessary to the story, but usually didn't have cast members. Sometimes these are called insert shots, like a close-up of a letter someone is reading, or a shot of shoes walking across the floor. These could be filmed with a second unit while Scorsese was filming something else.

As the visual effects supervisor, Rob was in charge of creating everything from a digital vision of Paris in 1931 to filming a spectacular train crash in miniature. Visual effects are often used in a film to depict things that may defy the laws of nature, reflect the world out of control, or are simply too large to be filmed "live."

Rob grew up in New Jersey, just outside of Asbury Park. "My very first movie was *Pinocchio*. I was probably as fascinated with the beam that projected the movie as I was with the movie itself. I kept looking back because I saw this flickering light, and even at four, I started trying to make a connection. It was sort of like the whole thing was a miracle.

"I always liked movies but I didn't know anything about the business. Then I picked up a book called *Memo from David O. Selznick*. The big chapter, the one everything was leading up to, was on *Gone with the Wind*. And I became absolutely fascinated with the idea that you should make something as good as it can possibly be."

The train crash Rob was in charge of filming really occurred in 1895, and I included the historical photo in my book. Perhaps he and his team could have created it with computer effects, like some other scenes in the movie, but Rob says, "My first instinct was to photograph it. I had experience photographing miniature models on the movies *Titanic* and *Apollo 13*. So we constructed the train and the window (in 1:4 scale), and it acted much like it did when the crash really occurred." The designers and engineers working on the shot spent four months creating the fifteen-foot-long train and the twenty-foot-tall station window. The miniature was pretty big! At the last minute Rob requested that miniature bikes and suitcases be added to the street below the window where the train would crash, so the model makers whipped those up in an hour or two! The crash itself, powered by an engine beneath the tracks, lasted a second and a half, but when it was projected on screen, they slowed it down, which adds to the illusion that this is a real train crashing through a gigantic window. Scorsese watched the filming of the crash via a computer link in New York City.

Thinking about his time on *Hugo*, as well as the book on David O. Selznick he'd read in his youth, Rob says, "Working now on a Selznick–Scorsese project is kind of a dream."

The fifteen-foot train as it crashes through the miniature façade of the train station. The day this scene was filmed, a twelve-year-old boy was visiting the set. He was allowed to say "Action!" which gave the cue to send the train speeding through the window.

Rob Legato transformed a lecture hall at the Sorbonne into this elegant Parisienne theater for Méliès's gala.

Joss Williams

SPECIAL EFFECTS

Joss Williams says his job "is to provide the physical effects for the movie, which are the effects that we shoot live on the set." For instance, Joss was in charge of building all the clocks with their infinite moving parts and making sure they were safe; he created ways to film the trains on the set so they looked real; and he provided all the steam, smoke, fire, and dust that fill the air. "We're shooting as much as we can on set in camera. It's always much better for the director and for the actors to be able to react and respond to something physically. For instance, we had massive, industrial steam boilers outside the set and piped the steam into the set. We also used different atmospheric smoke machines that look like steam, but it's cold."

Joss was born outside of London in a town called Taplow and flew to Holland when he was sixteen for his first special effects job on a movie called *A Bridge Too Far*. He's been in the business thirty-five years and knows lots of tricks of the trade. For instance, fake snow can be made from Epsom salts! "Also, if there's any really close shots where you've got people walking through the snow, we use a material that is used in baby's diapers. Once you put water into it, it looks like really good, slushy snow!"

Asa Butterfield (Hugo) is filmed as smoky atmosphere is pumped into the background.

Hugo (Asa Butterfield) behind the walls of the train station.

CHAPTER FIVE

FILMING BEGINS

Tim Monich

Tim Monich helps actors learn to speak their lines with the appropriate accents or dialects. "Long before production began on *Hugo*, there was some talk of having an international cast of American, English, and French actors. But as casting was confirmed, there were no French actors. We dropped the idea of French accents and instead chose a standard English. We decided on pronunciations that would be in English, but with a hint of French stress and rhythm.

"I had no childhood interest in accents or how people speak, but since my mother was a journalist and my father loved opera, words and music were a big part of my home in Corona, California. In elementary school I loved diagramming sentences. Taking apart the words and phrases is like opening up a watch or clock to see how it works.

"For over thirty-five years, I have made audio recordings of people talking. According to my iTunes, if you listened to all of the recordings, it would take fifty-nine-and-a-half days. These recordings are my chief tool for helping actors learn dialects and accents. I had Chloë Moretz listen to recordings I had made of four different English girls, and then I had her loosely imitate them. Working from that base, Chloë was free to create a way of talking that's just right for her character."

Tim Monich's pronunciation guide to help Chloë Moretz (one of the few cast members not from England) speak with an English accent. By reading the words on the left side of the page out loud, you can practice your English accent. The words on the right are other words that rhyme, to make sure the words are said correctly.

SCENE   PAGES   Dec. 9, 2010   Isabelle

20   13 - 15

hoo ah yoo?   OR   hoo uh yoo?

PAH-pa zhawzh isn't my grAnn-fah-thuh   band-lather   stand rather
and he izz'nt a theef.
he told me awl a-bowt yoo,   Is Paul a lout?   call a tout
yUng jEHntleman.   JEHN, not "gin"
                                                  Is your tongue gentle?
                                                  You're among lentils.
                                                  Where have they hung Yentl?
                                                  Kent'll manipulate

yaw nUthing but a ...
REPP-ra-bate!   Separate that reprobate!
                                                  Find Johnny Depp a mate.
                                                  Don't crepitate, you reprobate.
                                                  I caught a tetra, mate.

no. yoo haff-ta go.   Was NAFTA slow?
                                                  It was a BAFTA show.

wy do yoo need it so bAd-li?   heed it so sadly
                                                  feed it so gladly
                                                  lead it so madly

iz it a see-krit?   Is it a bee pit?
                                                  Is it a ski-knit?
                                                  Is it a FREE crit?

guud. i lUvv see-krits.   hood   stood   wood
tell me this inn-st'nt.

49   37 - 39

i dont noh. he nevvuh sed.   clever bed   sever lead
                                                  Trevor fled
I bet my peh^uh-r'nts wood've let me.   Sharon's   Karen's

Paul Kieve

ON SET MAGICIAN

Paul Kieve is a magician and illusion designer who did research and consulted with Martin Scorsese for the authentic magic effects performed in *Hugo*. He then supervised their construction, tutored the actors, and oversaw and advised as the magic was filmed. "When I first met Scorsese I did a show-and-tell. Working with both Sir Ben Kingsley and Asa Butterfield, I took cards along. I think it was quite tough for Asa's tutor those days I was on the set because it's like, 'Okay, it's magic lessons now. Would you rather do your math, or would you rather learn to impale a card on a sword?'"

Paul was born in East London and received a magic kit on his tenth birthday. "That had a big impact on me. I love the fact that I can honestly do some dishonest acts.

"Marty wanted magic that really would have been done in that time period, and I thought, wouldn't it be great if Méliès makes a card float up, and then Hugo tries to make his own version of the trick?

"When Sir Ben and Asa first met on set, we had this wonderful day where they did their magic stuff around the table. It was like, 'Oh, I can do this, and I can do this.' I wouldn't say there was a rivalry there, but there was definitely a bit of, you know, two magicians swapping techniques and skills."

Hugo (Asa Butterfield) and Georges Méliès
(Ben Kingsley) perform card tricks.

Mama Jeanne (Helen McCrory) levitating, with Georges Méliès (Ben Kingsley) in a flashback scene, filmed at the Athénée Théâtre Louis-Jouvet in Paris, France. Paul Kieve discovered an old poster illustrating a similar levitation trick and used it to help re-create this scene. Sandy Powell, the costume designer, handpainted the inside of the dress.

Doug Coleman

STUNT COORDINATOR

Doug Coleman is in charge of designing action sequences based on the characters and the story, and helping to tell that story so the action fits the spirit of the movie. Part of his job includes teaching the actors how to fall, jump, or run without getting injured. He also trains stunt doubles to stand in for the actors when the action is too dangerous. Chloë Moretz had to do some stunt work under Doug's supervision during a scene where she falls from a broken chair in the Mélièses' apartment. "We had a breakaway chair. Special effects triggered the chair to break — they pulled one of the legs out from under it so it collapses. We put a safety cable on Chloë so that when effects pulled the chair out, she dropped down into Asa's arms. We took most of her weight off her so Asa could catch her and lower her down to the ground. We probably broke about eleven or twelve chairs for that scene, for the different angles."

Doug grew up in Utah and one of his favorite movies was *The Absent-Minded Professor*. "How are these guys flying around a basketball court? They're actually up in the air? That's where I first saw wirework. Those things really sparked my interest from a technical standpoint of moviemaking. When I was eleven, I remember hooking up some ropes and flying from tree branch to tree branch." At fourteen, Doug and a friend hitchhiked to Los Angeles and snuck into a movie studio to watch films being made, and at eighteen, he went to Hollywood to stay.

During the shooting of *Hugo,* Doug worked a lot with Asa Butterfield because his character encounters many dangerous situations in the movie, including a hair-raising chase through Madame Emilie's café. "When I was dreaming this up, I had to put myself in a little kid's shoes. I ran through the café door and put people in front of me so I could hop up and over some seats. I ran it a few times and then we showed Martin Scorsese a rehearsal. Then I brought in Asa. We had to modify a few things to make it very safe for him to jump up and over the seats and tables. We changed his shoes out with non-skid soles, we put breakaways [dishes and cups that look like real china but will break harmlessly if you hit them] anywhere that was in his line. We padded tables. But he was so spot-on there were never any issues." Doug even used lots of Lemon Pledge to make the floor very slippery when Asa had to slide between Richard Griffiths' legs. And later in the chase, the Station Inspector has a very serious encounter with the café band. "It was Sacha's idea to stick his foot through the cello. We cut out the area that he was going to step through and replaced it with a very soft wood called balsa, and fine-tuned the edges to the point where they wouldn't hurt him at all. I think we went through no less than fifteen cellos."

The Station Inspector has a run-in with the café band. Doug Coleman, the stunt coordinator, made sure that no one — except the cello — was injured during filming.

Mathilde de Cagny

ANIMAL TRAINER

Mathilde de Cagny worked with Enzo, Blackie, and Borsalino, the three Doberman pinschers who played the Station Inspector's dog, Maximilian, and she also trained three dachshunds, who played the dogs owned by the characters Madame Emilie and Monsieur Frick. "Training an animal actor is not about tricks. You need to be able to read the animals and see what their fears are or what their needs are. In order to become a trainer, you must have patience, common sense, passion, and lots of good treats in your pocket."

Mathilde was born and raised in Paris, France. "I was constantly rescuing pigeons and any stray animals I could find. One day I saw a cat food commercial where a cat had to jump on a table and knock over a vase. This was the first time I realized someone trained that animal to do those behaviors.

"On *Hugo*, I had to be disguised as a character in many scenes, including once as a man with a mustache, in order to get the best camera angle and still be close enough to the animals to give them directions.

"The biggest problem I have between me and my husband is that I keep every animal that I work with. I have about seven dogs from *Hotel for Dogs* and from *Beverly Hills Chihuahua*. I live with a bunch of stars!"

Mathilde de Cagny, dressed as a man, waits with Blackie to film a scene in the train station.

The cat in Monsieur Labisse's bookshop.

Birds were also used in the movie. Here, two pigeons rest in the tower clock.

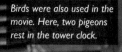

Martha Pinson

SCRIPT SUPERVISOR

Martha Pinson says that another name for her job is *continuity*. She is responsible for seeing that "every element: wardrobe, hair, makeup, special effects, camera, action, etc., matches from cut to cut." Because a movie is not filmed in order, one half of a scene might be filmed in September, and the second half of the same scene, or a scene that takes place earlier in the story, could be filmed months *later*. "An actor might ask me, 'Which way did I turn in the last take?' Or the prop person might ask, 'What time should be on the clock?' We keep an eye out for anything that is missed: a reaction, a beat, a decision, or a transition. We make notes to convey the director's comments to the editor. We note shot descriptions, line changes, and variations in the action."

Martha is from New Jersey. She spent many joyous hours doing math problems with her father, and seeing if she could beat him at chess. "I very much identified with the collaboration of Hugo and his father on the automaton. It gave Hugo a start on his life's work. That was a precious gift to him, as similar things were to me."

Now Martha uses those gifts every day on her job. "I have developed a skill for deep concentration. I seek to remember everything that is established on film, as the camera is rolling. The trick is to pay attention."

Martha Pinson's script with her notations. A line through the script represents each shot and what it covers. Solid lines mean on-camera dialogue, dotted lines mean off-camera. It's almost like a secret code between Martha and the editor Thelma Schoonmaker, who looks at these notations for information on how the movie can be edited.

                    HUGO
          How?

                    GEORGES
          Come to the booth everyday. I'll decide how long
          you must work for each item you stole, and it will
          be up to me to decide when you have earned your
          notebook, if ever.

                    HUGO
          I already have a job.

                    GEORGES
          Thief is not a job, boy.

                    HUGO
          I have another job, but I'll come when I can.

                    GEORGES
          You begin tomorrow. Go away.

                    HUGO
          I'll begin now.

          Hugo bravely goes into the booth and gets a broom.
          Starts sweeping up.

          Georges watches him.

          Across the station, a little DANCE BAND is starting up at
          Madame Emilie's cafe.

          A few couples dance.

          An afternoon tea dance.

          A lovely, bygone image. Couples dancing under the massive
          iron ribs of the great train station.

          The music echoes throughout the Grand Hall.

          The music from the band takes us to...

          INT./EXT. - MONTAGE - DAY/NIGHT

          Dance band music.

          ... Georges does a card trick. Hugo watches the trick
          closely. Georges notices.

The tea dance was one of the most complicated scenes for Martha Pinson to keep track of because so many things were going on at once. Hugo was watching from the toy shop, Isabelle was dancing with her friends, other characters were chatting inside the café, and the orchestra was playing.

Thelma Schoonmaker

EDITOR

Thelma Schoonmaker explains that "an editor takes the raw footage shot each day and shapes it into dramatic scenes by carefully choosing (along with the director) the best performances of the actors, and the best camera work. How long an actor's face is on the screen, or whether the line he speaks is heard over someone else's face instead, how quickly or slowly a scene is cut, these are all the job of an editor working closely with the director, composer, and sound editors. I begin editing as soon as I am given the first day's shooting. You have to live with a film for some months before you really know what is right. We screen the film many times and often make changes right up to the last minute.

"It took a long time for me to learn about editing. I never thought I would become a filmmaker. I wanted to become a diplomat. Both my parents were American, but my father worked for an oil company and I was born in Algeria. I then grew up on the island of Aruba in the Caribbean. My parents gave me a love of music and painting and books. I saw Michael Powell's film *The Red Shoes* when I was twelve and it affected me deeply. My family returned to the United States when I was fifteen. I took a film course one summer at New York University and that's where I met Martin Scorsese. He actually taught me all I have ever known about editing. I was twenty-two when I first started working with him, and I am still learning from him today.

"Scorsese and I have a very long collaboration and work very intensely together on the editing. We eat in the editing room; we never go out to lunch. We don't argue, but we discuss different opinions constantly. Scorsese has extremely high standards, and believe me there is nothing more wonderful to be around than that. He always sets himself a new challenge when he makes a film, and I get to be challenged along with him. But sometimes when we are frustrated by a scene, the best thing to do is turn off the editing equipment and go home and come back in the next day with a fresh mind."

Like much of the crew, *Hugo* was Thelma's first experience working with 3-D. "Technically, the 3-D was challenging, but it didn't take too long to learn about it. Certainly you have to be careful about too much quick cutting. Scorsese and Bob Richardson, our cameraman, have been very inventive with the use of 3-D.

"There is an extra TV monitor off to the side in the editing room and classic movies run on it all day, with the sound turned off so as not to distract us. But it is very inspiring to glance over every now and then and be enriched by what we see."

Martin Scorsese and Thelma Schoonmaker discuss a scene. Thelma says, "I love to visit the set and watch Scorsese work. We have worked for many years with the same crew, and we are old friends. But my job as an editor is to have a cold eye when I see the footage shot every day. It's better not to have any preconceived notions and see things fresh."

INSPECTOR NABS STREET KID - PT. 1		
INSPECTOR NABS STREET KID - PT. 2		
INSPECTOR ASKS POLICE TO TAKE KID		
POLICE TAKE KID		
TEA DANCE - HUGO WATCHES ISABELLE FROM TUNNEL		
HUGO ASKS ISABELLE TO THE MOVIES		
ARRIVE MOVIE THEATRE		
HUGO PICKS LOCK		
THEY WATCH "SAFETY LAST"		
MANAGER THROWS THEM OUT		
THEY LEARN ABOUT EACH OTHER REEL		
INSPECTOR STOPS THEM		
HUGO & ISABELLE LUGGAGE ROOM		
HUGO DISCOVERS KEY REEL		
ISABELLE TO APARTMENT		
AUTOMATON DRAWS REEL		
ISABELLE BRINGS HUGO HOME		
JEANNE UPSET BY DRAWING		
HUGO & ISABELLE HIDE IN BEDROOM		
ISABELLE FINDS BOX		
GEORGES HAUNTED		
ISABELLE THANKS HUGO REEL		
LABISSE GIVES HUGO BOOK		
INSPECTOR / LISETTE CONNECT		
LABISSE SUGGESTS FILM ACADEMY		
HUGO & ISABELLE TO FILM ACADEMY		
FILM ACADEMY LIBRARY LOBBY		
FIND BOOK IN LIBRARY REEL		
CLIP - TRAIN ARRIVES		

	#	Scene
	62B	CLIPS - 1ST MOVIES THRU RENOIR
	63	TABARD'S SHRINE TO GEORGES
	64	FLASHBACK: TABARD AT GEORGES' STUDIO
	65	FLASHBACK: WATCHES GEORGES WORK - FAIRIES
	65A	FLASHBACK: FILM PROCESSED
12	66	TABARD REVEALS FILM CANISTER REEL
	67	HANGING CLOCK - DROPS WRENCH
	68	HUGO & ISABELLE DISCUSS THEIR PURPOSE
	69	LOOK OUT OVER PARIS (VFX - SOLAR SYSTEM)
	70	HUGO TELLS ISABELLE HIS PLAN
	71	GEORGES AND ISABELLE LEAVE STATION
	72	HUGO GOES TO SLEEP
	73	HUGO'S NIGHTMARE - TRAIN CRASHES
	73B	HUGO AS AUTOMATON
13	74	HUGO WAKES UP REEL
	75	UNCLE CLAUDE'S BODY DISCOVERED
	76	HUGO LEADS TABARD TO GEORGES
	77	TABARD SHOWS TRIP TO THE MOON
	78	FLASHBACK: MAGIC ACT
14	79	FLASHBACK: GEORGES & AUTOMATON REEL
	80	FLASHBACK: SEE FLICKERING LIGHT
	81	FLASHBACK: GEORGES AND JEANNE TRANSPORTED
	82	FLASHBACK: GEORGES BUILDS MOVIE CAMERA
	83	FLASHBACK: GEORGES & JEANNE POSE FOR PHOTO

	#	Scene
	84A	FLASHBACK: GEORGES SKETCHES COSTUME
	84B	FLASHBACK: YOUNG JEANNE FITTED
	84C	FLASHBACK: GEORGES PAINTS SCENERY
	84D	FLASHBACK: FAUST TRAP DOOR
	84E	FLASHBACK: JEANNE WIPES OFF SOOT
	84F	FLASHBACK: DRAGON
	84G	FLASHBACK: TRICK SHOT - SKELETONS
	84H	FLASHBACK: FILM EDITED
	84I	FLASHBACK: SPLICED TRICK SHOT - VFX
	84J	FLASHBACK: YOUNG JEANNE AS CONSTELLATION
	84K	FIREWORKS SURROUND HER
	84L	WWI EXPLOSION
	85	MOVIE POSTERS WASH AWAY
	86	GEORGES IN MOVIE THEATRE
	87	TIME-LAPSE - STUDIO DECAYS
	88	GEORGES DESTROYS SETS
	88A	CELLULOID TURNED INTO SHOE HEEL
	89	GEORGES IN TOY SHOP - LOST
	90	HUGO "NOT OVER YET"
15	91	HUGO RACES TO TRAIN STATION REEL
	91A	HUGO ON ROOFTOPS
	92	INSPECTOR NABS HUGO
	93	HUGO ESCAPES CELL
	94	HUGO EVADES INSPECTOR
	95	HUGO DISAPPEARS
	96	HUGO ON TURNTABLE
	97	HUGO CLIMBS TO TOWER CLOCK

	#	Scene
	98	INSPECTOR FOLLOWS
	99	HUGO CLIMBS THRU CLOCK FACE
	99A	HUGO HANGS ON CLOCK - "SAFETY LAST"
16	100	HUGO EVADES BACKGUARDS REEL
	101	HUGO AT TRAIN - SEES INSPECTOR
	102	HUGO CORNERED
	103	HUGO SAVES AUTOMATON
	104	GEORGES CONFRONTS INSPECTOR
	105	GEORGES HONORED FOR HIS FILMS
	106	HUGO PERFORMS CARD TRICKS

Thelma Schoonmaker's editing suite. On screen you can see the interior of a movie theater in Hugo. The wall is covered with Thelma's storyboard, which indicates how many scenes there are, and in which order they go.

Howard Shore

COMPOSER

Howard Shore wrote the score for the movie. He composed music that helps build the excitement or reveals the emotions of the story. Regarding his work on *Hugo*, he says, "In the beginning of the movie, seven themes are introduced, including a mystery theme; Hugo's theme, which at first is a bit playful and optimistic, but also bold; and the Station Inspector's theme, which will be one of pursuit, with a bit of military clumsiness and humor. The themes are used for clarity of storytelling and they develop over the course of the film. They are the foundation from which the entire score can grow."

Howard says his earliest memories of music are singing in school each morning. His favorite movies as a kid included everything from *Treasure Island* to the epic *The Ten Commandments*. Some of the instruments Howard uses in *Hugo* include a musette (a French accordion), an ondes martenot (a French theremin), a small 1930s drum kit, an alto saxophone, and a vintage gypsy jazz guitar.

Howard says, "I want to match the depth of the sound to the depth of the image. I would like the score to sound like the imagery. A marriage of light and sound."

Howard Shore's first musical notations for the score. The mystery theme plays when the automaton is discovered.

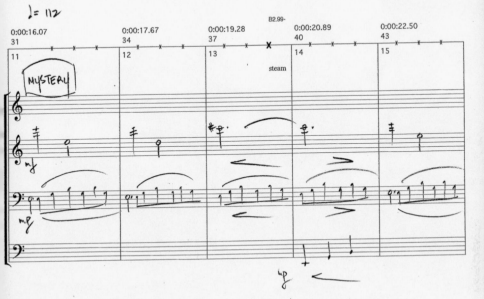

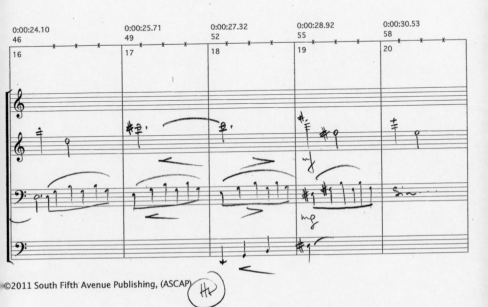

Ben Kingsley (Georges Méliès) and Helen McCrory (Mama Jeanne) during filming of the party scene.

CHAPTER SIX

THE
PARTY

THE FINAL SHOT

WE'VE NOW MET ALL THE MAIN PLAYERS
in the making of this movie and we've learned about
their jobs. Individually, each person plays a critical role,
but what is remarkable is the way this brilliant team of
artists and technicians, led by Martin Scorsese, works
together. Every frame of the entire movie is the result of
months and months of conversations, questions, deci-
sions, and discoveries. For the last chapter of this book,
I thought it would be interesting to take a close look at
how they collaborated on *one single scene*. And what better scene than the amazing final two minutes of the film?

Before we begin, let's revisit my original book. Even
though John Logan stuck very close to my story, for
many reasons, I knew the ending would have to change.
John decided to focus the last scene on a moment
inspired by a party that happens right after the Méliès
gala at the French Film Academy. In the original book,
this moment was not very important, and it's described
almost in passing:

> *After the gala ended, they all went to a small party
> in [Méliès's] honor at a nearby restaurant. Isabelle took
> photographs the entire night, and Hugo sat at a table
> doing magic tricks.*
>
> *A rather sizable crowd soon gathered around Hugo. . . .*

John decided to move the party from the "nearby restaurant" to the Méliès apartment. "I always knew I wanted to end the script with Hugo happily at home with his new 'family.' For me that's what the movie is about: how a sad orphan finds his way home. It seemed like a fun idea to show all the characters celebrating together, a real happy ending."

In the script, John describes Isabelle entering the party with a notebook and pen, then sitting in a chair and starting to write down the story that we've all just watched on screen. In a voice-over, we hear what she is writing. "I thought Isabelle writing the story of Hugo's adventure would give the character a sense of arriving at her destiny like Hugo does," said John, referring to a conversation the children have about what their purpose in life might be. "I wanted both Hugo and Isabelle to be stepping into their future, like in Brian's book."

When creating a shot like this, every single detail needs to be worked out ahead of time so nothing goes wrong during the filming. Martin Scorsese says, "When I first read the scene, I realized it would have to be in one shot (with no cuts). I discussed this with the whole production crew. We all discussed logistics and made alterations before the set was built. Then with Chris Surgent, I worked on creating little bits of business for each character. We worked on each character's place-ment — we knew the shot had to start on one person and then end on the automaton's face.

"Because it is a complicated shot, involving not only all of the major characters in the film but extra children, a band of musicians, and dogs, we needed to rehearse it so that we didn't waste any time on the day of filming."

A month before filming the scene, Chris Surgent began those rehearsals. As he worked on blocking the shot with Scorsese, using stand-ins in place of the actors, he says, "First, we had to figure out a way that Larry McConkey's Steadicam could circle Chloë as she sat in the corner of the room. The problem was that the rig was too large to get between her and the walls of the room. You could move her farther out in the room, but then it would appear as if she were sitting too far away from the corner. To solve this, the wall behind Chloë could be pulled away during the camera move, once it was out of shot, and another mechanism could slide Chloë's chair forward, creating enough space for the Steadicam."

The set was constructed without a ceiling so lights could be hung from above. Meanwhile, the costume team, headed by Sandy Powell, was creating all the costumes for the final scene. Sandy says, "Apart from the flashback scenes, this scene was the only opportunity to see any of the characters in different clothing from their everyday wear. Having said that, I still wanted to maintain elements already established with each character."

Two days before the shoot was finally to take place, I visited the set. David Davenport, the costume supervisor, told me he'd just gotten notice that they needed about ten more extras for the last scene. He asked if I would like to be in the movie. Of course, I said yes! I was going to have my own cameo! Before I knew what was happening, I was in the extras' tent, having a costume fitting with Tim Aslam, the assistant costume designer, who picked out a beautiful suit for me to wear. Next I was brought to the makeup department at the other end of the tent, and I was neatly shaved before being whisked upstairs to have my hair cut by Jan Archibald. She gave me a nifty 1930s style. Once I was done, I was told that in order to be employed by the movie (appearing as an extra would make me an employee), I must leave the country and re-enter with special working papers, which would need to be stamped on my way back to England.

At 7:30 the next morning, I found myself on the Eurostar, the underground train to Paris. I arrived in the Gare du Nord, the station on which I based much of Hugo's station. It was cold outside, and I don't speak French, and suddenly I realized that I didn't want to be in the *real* Paris at all, I wanted to be in *my* Paris, the one that Dante Ferretti had built in Shepperton Studios in London. So within forty-five minutes, with my papers stamped, I was on my way back to the Paris I'd imagined.

The morning of the shoot, the extras changed into their costumes in the huge tent and all the principal actors prepared in their private dressing rooms. I was given my own dressing room, too, and I changed into my costume. Morag Ross and Kate Benton, the key makeup artist, started getting everyone ready very early that morning, and it took about four hours to do all of the makeup. Everyone was made to look fresh and clean. I was given a shave and a little bit of color around my eyes. It also took Jan Archibald, the hair designer, and her team four hours to do the fancy hair for this scene, including a little trim for me. A small silver clip was put in my hair to keep it in place until filming began.

When we were all ready, we walked to the vast soundstage where the preparations were under way for the big shoot. We passed through the graveyard, the French street, the apartment building, and walked upstairs to the second floor where the Méliès apartment was waiting. I felt like I had really traveled back in time to Paris in 1931.

David Balfour and his team got the automaton ready for its close-up. Having made fifteen different versions, the one for the party was the shiniest and most beautiful of them all. It had the final, enigmatic smile that would complete the transformation from the sad ruins of the burned machine to the contented, gleaming, silver automaton now waiting in the corner of the bedroom. A team of technicians drilled a hole in the wall for access to the automaton, just in case Scorsese decided at the last minute he wanted it to be able to move. Even though everything is planned ahead, everyone also tries to be ready for last-minute changes. For instance, the costume department made a miniature tuxedo for the automaton to wear during the party scene, but it was removed by Scorsese, who wanted us to be able to see all of its shining machinery.

The extras huddled around some heat lamps on the ground floor, trying to stay warm because it was very cold that morning, and the huge doors to the soundstage didn't keep out the chill. Nearby, a semicircle of director's chairs for the principal actors surrounded a few more heat lamps. Sir Christopher Lee and Richard Griffiths took their seats. They were in full costume, but had thick down jackets on as well. Emily Mortimer, Frances de la Tour, and Sacha Baron Cohen arrived. Meanwhile, up in the Méliès apartment, dozens of people scurried around, arranging the lights, moving cables, and trying to get ready for the shoot. Several black tents were set up, and inside the tents, 3-D monitors were plugged in. Chairs were placed in front of the monitors, along with trays of snacks for the crew. The 3-D stereographer, Demetri Portelli, settled into his tent, ready to do his work. Another tent nearby was prepared for Scorsese and those closest to him, like Martha Pinson, the script supervisor, who was watching to see that they didn't miss a beat or a line, and Chris Surgent, who would be running the rehearsal. The whole crew had their own 3-D glasses, which they kept in their pockets, around their necks, or clipped onto their regular glasses.

I was very nervous. I had never been in a movie before. I worried that I'd shake, or I'd accidentally look at the camera and ruin the shot. While all these thoughts were going through my head, Chris Surgent came up to me with some paper in his hand. "Here's your script," he said. "Memorize your line. We start rehearsing in a few minutes."

My line? I didn't know I was going to have a line. I thought I was going to throw up! I was being asked to play "Eager Student," and my line was, "When can I sign up?" Luckily, it's an easy line to memorize. You've probably memorized it already.

Chris led me upstairs along with the other actors and the extras, and we carefully stepped over all the camera and light cables until we got to the set. Now that everything had been blocked out, Chris spent the morning teaching all the actors in the scene where we should go. Before I knew it, I was crammed into the tiny kitchen at the far end of the hallway with Michael Stuhlbarg and Sir Ben Kingsley. Another extra, Tomos Owain James, soon joined us, and we rehearsed running down the hallway to the living room where the party was going on. In the script, Méliès and Tabard are having a conversation about a class that Méliès will be teaching in the fall at the French Film Academy, but the actors and the crew soon realized that Michael and Sir Ben didn't have enough lines to fill the time it takes to get from the kitchen to the living room. A conference was held with Scorsese, and Michael was given a new line on the spot. His line was much harder to memorize than mine. He had to discuss the thaumatrope, the zoetrope, and the praxinoscope (devices that predate the camera)! Once the lines were added, Martha Pinson made sure to mention the new text to the people recording the sound so they would know to cue for it.

Asa practiced the two magic tricks he'd been taught by Paul Kieve for this scene, and Chloë practiced walking to the chair, sitting, and beginning to write while the small platform the chair rested on was moved forward to accommodate Larry's camera. The tech crew rehearsed moving the wall away at the right time so no one would see it on screen. Mathilde, the dog trainer (now in costume because she was going to be visible on camera), sat with Blackie the dog and got her ready for the scene. Richard Griffiths, Frances de la Tour, and Sir Christopher Lee rehearsed their lines together, and Sacha Baron Cohen and Emily Mortimer practiced their lines and their movement from the chair by the fireplace to the corner of the living room where a small band would be playing. Sacha had a new shiny brass leg brace to wear.

Emil Lager, playing the guitarist Django Reinhardt, walked across the living room strumming his guitar, and tech guys dressed like party guests rehearsed moving tables and credenzas to allow the cameras to pass by. Sir Ben, Michael, Tomos, and I practiced our entrance, and when we ran into the party room and stopped in front of Helen, I had to turn to my left and say my line to Sir Ben, at which point the camera was next to me on my right. As it moved past me, Chris told me to push myself up against Sir Ben so there would be room for the camera to get by me. I was surprised to discover that all the actors remained in character throughout the scene, even when we were squished up against one another and the camera could not see us.

A little while later, Michael and I were given something else to do as well. Toward the end of the scene, we would have to carefully step over the camera cables when no one was looking and move across the hall to the doorway of the bedroom. We were asked to lean against the wall with our drinks, make up a conversation, and laugh as the camera glides past us into the bedroom toward the automaton, and the end of the shot.

After several hours of rehearsal, everyone knew exactly what they had to do, and it was time to start filming. Scorsese was ready with his 3-D glasses in his black tent. As we took our places to begin, Tim Monich, the dialect coach, came up to me and said, "You know you have to do this with an English accent, right?" No, I did not know that! Tim said, "Let me hear your English accent." So I said my line with my fake English accent. He said it wasn't bad but gave me some suggestions to make it sound more authentic. I tried it a few more times, Tim said it sounded good, and off he went!

While we waited to hear the word *Action*, which would signal everyone to start, Sir Ben, Michael, Tomos, and I all huddled in the tiny kitchen at the far end of the hallway. There were no other scenes in this room, but the set decorators had still created a fully functional 1930s kitchen. We opened the cabinets and found real food inside. Sir Ben offered to make a soup.

It was now time to start filming. If anything went wrong, we'd have to stop the whole scene, set up the shot again, and begin once more. I wasn't really nervous because Sir Ben and Michael are so brilliant that I realized during rehearsals all I would have to do is follow along and just listen to them.

There were thirty-three people acting in front of the camera and two hundred and forty people working behind the scenes that day. When everyone was ready, Scorsese shouted, "Action!" Larry, on a crane above the set, swooped in toward the open space where the window would be, carefully stepped off the crane, and entered the hallway. Extras were taking off their coats, opening and closing doors, and talking to one another. From the other end of the hallway, Méliès, Tabard, Tomos, and I burst from the kitchen as Méliès and Tabard eagerly discussed the new class that Méliès would be teaching at the Film Academy in the fall. As we turned left into the party room, the camera caught up with us and followed us in. We passed Hugo doing a card trick for a small group of people and Tomos joined this group. But Tabard, Méliès, and I continued on, stopping to talk with Mama Jeanne, who was signing an autograph for a fan. I said my line ("When can I sign up?") and as the camera passed us, I squished against Méliès like I was supposed to. The camera followed Isabelle, who had entered behind us. She watched Hugo do a magic trick, then took her seat in the chair. The wall moved, the credenza was rolled to the side, and the chair slid forward as the camera moved around her. Then it passed Monsieur Labisse, Madame Emilie, and Monsieur Frick as they talked. The prop guys, dressed as party guests, moved the center table out of the way so the camera could pass. The Station Inspector, wearing his new brass leg brace, with his dog at his side, talked to Lisette, and then the three of them got up and crossed over to the band, which was playing music along with Django. The Station Inspector and Lisette waltzed beside Méliès and Mama Jeanne as the camera glided past them, through the doors and into the hallway, where Tabard and I were leaning against the bedroom door frame, talking and laughing with drinks in our hands. The camera continued past us into the bedroom, slowly moving closer to the automaton, which was shining in the moonlight. The camera kept going until it zoomed in on the automaton's face and Scorsese yelled, "Cut!"

At least that's what was supposed to happen. It seemed like something was always going wrong. Either an actor would forget a line, or the wall would move too soon, or Larry would accidentally walk into a doorway at the very last minute, but none of this was unusual. These were all the sorts of mistakes that happen when you are filming a scene of this length and complexity.

After filming the entire shot twelve times, Scorsese said he got what he needed and everyone cheered and hugged. It felt like a very big accomplishment. Then we all gathered around Sir Christopher Lee because it was his last day of filming. Scorsese said a few words and then Sir Christopher told us how much this experience had meant to him.

Later, the special effects would be added, creating the window through which the camera first enters, and then the city of Paris, visible behind the automaton. Chloë would record the text that would play as a voice-over. And when it was time to edit the movie, Thelma Schoonmaker and Scorsese would choose from the two perfect shots we'd done that day. All of that work, every decision and detail, was for two minutes of film.

Eventually Thelma and Scorsese cut together 103 scenes, from 135 hours of film, with 28 principal actors and over 500 extras. Howard Shore, hoping the depth of the sound would match the depth of the images in 3-D, composed a score that was played by 94 musicians. At Shepperton Studios, the filmmakers needed 100 miles of electric cable for the train station set alone. The lighting used 750 large hanging lamps and 3,100,000 watts, which is equivalent to 50,000 sixty-watt lightbulbs.

There were 34 prop builders, 15 automatons, 144 set builders, 60 different sets, 40 costume assistants, hundreds of costumes, 15 people on makeup, 13 on hair, 50 on electrics, 17 on the cameras, 42 working on miniatures in Los Angeles, and hundreds of others all over the world who contributed in one way or another to the making of *Hugo*.

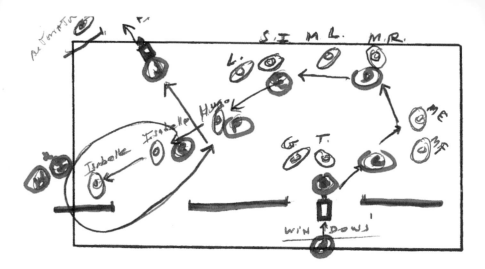

Martin Scorsese's original storyboards for the filming of
the party scene. The arrows indicate camera movement.

Getting my hair cut the morning of the party scene.

Technicians adjust the Station Inspector's leg brace as Emily Mortimer (Lisette) looks on. A brand-new leg brace was constructed for this scene as if Hugo and Méliès had built it for the Inspector.

Michael Stuhlbarg (René Tabard), and I (Eager Student, with silver hair clip keeping a cowlick in place before filming), listen to the director Martin Scorsese.

Martin Scorsese goes over the script with Frances de la Tour (Madame Emilie) as Richard Griffiths (Monsieur Frick) listens nearby.

The party scene being filmed. Note the crew, in costume, on the left side, moving the central table out of the way for the Steadicam.

Another view of the party scene being filmed. You can see Larry McConkey with the Steadicam in the corner of the room behind Chloë Moretz (Isabelle) sitting in the chair. Also note the wall behind Larry, which has moved to make room for him.

WINDING IT UP

TIME CAN PLAY ALL SORTS OF TRICKS ON YOU. In the blink of an eye, ideas turn into books; automatons shudder, click, and draw mysterious pictures; children run through crowds; and movies flicker to life on a million shining screens around the world.

That's what happened to Hugo Cabret, a character whose name I'd taken from a toy I'd loved as a kid, and a French word I'd made up one day at my desk. Watching the movie now, I think about myself as a child drawing day and night, and I think about Martin Scorsese in the cinema with his father, and Thelma Schoonmaker growing up in Aruba, and John Logan watching Laurence Olivier as Hamlet, and Dante Ferretti sitting in a clock tower in Italy. I marvel at the long, unexpected twists and turns that led us here . . . children from all over the world who grew up and came together to collaborate on a movie about two lonely kids who find their purpose in a train station in Paris.

THE END

POSTSCRIPT

If you enjoyed learning about my book and Martin Scorsese's movie and are interested in continuing to discover the world of Hugo Cabret, read on. . . .

Adventures in Paris

THE MUSÉE D'ORSAY — This museum built in an old train station houses two clocks featured in my book. In the main room, over the entrance, you'll see the clock where Hugo looks out from the number 5, and if you go up to the café, you'll see the glass clock I used when Hugo and Isabelle talk about their purpose. *1 Rue de la Légion d'Honneur, 75007 Paris*, www.musee-orsay.fr/en/home.html

THE CINÉMATHÈQUE FRANÇAISE — Here you will find a wonderful collection of original Méliès artifacts, including the robe that Méliès wore in *A Trip to the Moon*. I used that same robe for Méliès at the end my book. *51 Rue de Bercy, 75012 Paris*, www.cinematheque.fr

MUSÉE GRÉVIN — This is the world's oldest wax museum (they have a figure of Georges Méliès!), and it has an amazing hall of mirrors you won't forget. *10 Boulevard Montmartre, 75009 Paris*, www.grevin.com/home

MUSÉE DES AUTOMATES — This museum is dedicated to magic and automatons. *11 Rue Saint Paul, 75004 Paris*, www.museedesautomates.fr

PÈRE-LACHAISE — Méliès is buried in this cemetery, and it is worth a trip. *6 Rue du Repos, 75020 Paris*, www.pere-lachaise.com

CIMETIÈRE MONTPARNASSE — This is the cemetery near Méliès's home. *3 Boulevard Edgar-Quinet, 75014 Paris*, www.pariscemeteries.com/pages/montparnasse.html

SORBONNE — The Méliès Film Academy gala was shot here. *1 Rue Victor Cousin, 75005 Paris*, www.english.paris-sorbonne.fr

BIBLIOTHÈQUE SAINTE-GENEVIÈVE — The Film Academy Library was filmed here, across from the Pantheon. *10 place du Pantheon, 75005 Paris*, www-bsg.univ-paris1.fr/home.htm

ATHÉNÉE THÉÂTRE LOUIS-JOUVET — This is the exterior of the Paris Cinema; the magic levitation scene in the flashback was shot inside. *Square de l'Opéra Louis-Jouvet, 7 Rue Boudreau, 75009 Paris*, www.athenee-theatre.com

Adventures in New York City

GRAND CENTRAL TERMINAL — The secret rooms and apartments hidden above the magnificent starry ceiling inspired part of my story. *87 East 42nd Street, New York, NY 10017*, www.grandcentralterminal.com

THE NEW YORK PUBLIC LIBRARY PICTURE COLLECTION — Mid-Manhattan

Library, *455 Fifth Avenue (at 40th Street), 3rd floor, New York, NY 10016,* www.nypl.org

MUSEUM OF THE MOVING IMAGE — Learn all about the history of cinema! *36-01 35 Avenue, Astoria, NY 11106,* www.movingimage.us

Other Fun Websites

The Méliès family site, for those who speak French — www.melies.eu
The Franklin Institute, home of the Maillardet automaton — www2.fi.edu
Michael Start's automaton website — www.automatomania.co.uk
The official website of my book, *The Invention of Hugo Cabret* — www.theinventionofhugocabret.com
Paramount's website to learn more about the movie — www.paramount.com

Movies That Inspired The Invention of Hugo Cabret

Les quatre cents coups (*The 400 Blows*), director François Truffaut, 1959
L'Atalante, director Jean Vigo, 1934
Le million (*The Million*), director René Clair, 1931
Sous les toits de Paris (*Under the Roofs of Paris*), director René Clair, 1930
Zéro de conduite (*Zero for Conduct*), director Jean Vigo, 1933
Le voyage dans la lune (*A Trip to the Moon*) and all of Georges Méliès's films, 1902, etc.

Movies Martin Scorsese Showed His Cast and Crew

(For 3-D)
House of Wax, director Andre de Toth, 1953
Dial "M" for Murder, director Alfred Hitchcock, 1954
Kiss Me Kate, director George Sidney, 1953
These movies can only be seen at special theaters in 3-D but are available on DVD in 2-D.
(Silent Films)
Lumière Brothers' movies
(For Color Tinting)
At the Villa Rose, director Maurice Elvey, 1920
The Great White Silence, director Herbert G. Ponting, 1924
(For Enjoyment)
The Fallen Idol, director Carol Reed, 1948. A mystery story about a young boy who lives in a big embassy and thinks he sees a murder.
A Kid for Two Farthings, director Carol Reed, 1955. The story of a poor boy in London and a unicorn.
The Magic Box, director John Boulting, 1952. The moving story of William Friese-Greene, who was one of the first to invent the motion picture camera.
These three British films are available on DVD.

BIOGRAPHIES

JAN ARCHIBALD (Hair Designer), a distinguished hairdresser and designer, has worked on feature and TV films in Britain and the US during the last several decades. Her credits include *A Private Function* and *The Shooting Party* through *Sense and Sensibility* and *Stars Wars: Episode I—The Phantom Menace* to, more recently, the HBO series *John Adams*, and *The Damned United*. Ms. Archibald received a 2007 Academy Award for her makeup design on *La Vie en Rose*.

DAVID BALFOUR (Props Master) worked at the Citizen's Theater in Glasgow, Scotland, his hometown, before starting work in the movies. Career highlights include *Michael Collins*, *Evita*, *The Butcher Boy*, *Alexander*, and *Sweeney Todd: The Demon Barber of Fleet Street*.

MARIANNE BOWER (Researcher) graduated from Oberlin College with Honors in English and lived briefly in England as part of a performing group "Musica Humana." In New York, she worked on the PBS series *Great Performances*, including programs for *Dance in America*. Some of her other credits include *George Balanchine's The Nutcracker* and *The Balanchine Essays*. She met Thelma Schoonmaker in the mid-1990s and began working on the archive of British filmmaker Michael Powell. In 1999, Ms. Bower met Martin Scorsese when she worked on his documentary *Il Mio Viaggio in Italia*, becoming his researcher and paper archivist in 2001.

JAAP BUITENDIJK (Stills Photographer), was born in Holland, and attended university in the UK. Jaap's many film credits as stills photographer include *Gladiator*, *Girl with a Pearl Earring*, *Alexander*, *Children of Men*, *In Bruges*, *Harry Potter and the Half-Blood Prince*, *Harry Potter and the Deathly Hallows* (Parts 1 and 2), and many others.

ASA BUTTERFIELD (Hugo Cabret) has been a professional actor since he was eight years old. After small roles in the British movie *Son of Rambow* and the British television drama *After Thomas*, he played the lead in the movie *The Boy in the Striped Pajamas*.

Since then, Asa has been in the movies *Wolfman* and *Nanny McPhee Returns*, and on TV in *Ashes to Ashes* and *Merlin*. Although busy with acting and his regular training at Young Actors Theatre in London, Asa makes a point of not letting it dominate his life. He enjoys school, friends, piano, squash, and his cats. He is just as happy reading a book as playing computer games. His favorite authors include Darren Shan and Anthony Horowitz.

DOUG COLEMAN (Stunt Coordinator) was born and raised in Salt Lake City, Utah. He has been coordinating stunts in films for over thirty years. His numerous credits include *Star Trek: Nemesis*, *A.I. Artificial Intelligence*, *Robo Cop*, *Married to the Mob*, *Batman Forever*, *The Perfect Storm*, *The Road to Perdition*, *Spider-Man 2*, and most recently *Men in Black III*, among many others. Doug coordinated stunts for Martin Scorsese's *Cape Fear* and *Casino*.

He recently directed second unit on the upcoming *Captain America*.

GUSTAVE DASTÉ (The Station Inspector) fought in the Great War, where he was decorated, though not necessarily for bravery. A stern disciplinarian, renowned for the apprehension of stray animals and orphans, the Inspector is also an expert at always knowing when the station's clocks are running slow. He lives in Paris with his companion, Maximilian (the Doberman), and is visited regularly by his sweetheart, Lisette (the flower seller).

MATHILDE DE CAGNY (Animal Trainer) was born in Paris, France, and moved to Los Angeles at the age of twenty. One of her first professional jobs was to tend to the stars of the live animal show at Universal Studios Hollywood. Shortly after, Ms. de Cagny rescued a mutt named Fred who was hired to play Einstein in the *Back to the Future* sequel. Her other notable credits with canines include *Frasier*, *As Good As It Gets*, *My Dog Skip*, *Lassie*, *Hotel for Dogs*, and *Marley and Me*.

FRANCES DE LA TOUR (Madame Emilie) trained at the Drama Centre London from 1961 to 1964, before joining the Royal Shakespeare Company, where her work included Helena in Peter Brook's production of *A Midsummer Night's Dream*.

Ms. de la Tour's other work for the theater includes the title role in *Hamlet* and Noël Coward's *Fallen Angels*. She won a Tony Award for her performance in *The History Boys* when it played on Broadway. Her film appearances include *Harry Potter and the Goblet of Fire* (playing Madame Olympe Maxime), *The History Boys*, and Tim Burton's *Alice in Wonderland*.

DANTE FERRETTI (Production Designer), winner of two Academy Awards, makes his eighth film for Martin Scorsese with *Hugo*. He previously designed *The Age of Innocence*, *Casino*, *Kundun*, *Bringing Out the Dead*, *Gangs of New York*, *Shutter Island*, and *The Aviator*, for which he was honored with his first Oscar.

Mr. Ferretti has also collaborated with the directors Julie Taymor (*Titus*), Franco Zeffirelli (*Hamlet*), Terry Gilliam (*Baron Munchausen*), and Jean-Jacques Annaud (*The Name of the Rose*). He has designed five films for Pier Paolo Pasolini and five for Federico Fellini. He won his second Oscar for Tim Burton's *Sweeney Todd: The Demon Barber of Fleet Street*.

Mr. Ferretti has also designed for such prestigious opera houses as Milan's La Scala, Teatro Colón in Buenos Aires, Teatro Roma Opera, and Paris's Bastille Opera House.

RICHARD GRIFFITHS (Monsieur Frick) is one of England's most versatile and distinguished stage and screen actors, having recently been seen in *Harry Potter and the Deathly Hallows* (his fifth appearance in the saga as Uncle Vernon). Other film credits include *Pirates of the Caribbean: On Stranger Tides*, *Sleepy Hollow*, *Superman II*, *Naked Gun 2*, *Gandhi*, *Ragtime*, *The History Boys*, and *Chariots of Fire*.

On stage, Mr. Griffiths has been celebrated for his work in shows such as

Equus, The Man Who Came to Dinner, and *The History Boys*, winning a Tony Award when he played the lead role on Broadway.

TIM HEADINGTON (Producer), together with longtime friend and colleague Graham King, formed the Los Angeles-based production company GK Films in 2007. Under the GK banner, he and King produced the upcoming films *The Rum Diary*, and *In the Land of Blood and Honey*. Their previous productions include *The Tourist, Edge of Darkness,* and *The Young Victoria*.

Outside of GK Films, Headington was also an executive producer on Gore Verbinski's animated adventure *Rango*, and on the upcoming film *Dark Shadows*. GK Films recently announced several new projects that Headington will produce, including the untitled Freddie Mercury story starring Sacha Baron Cohen being written by Peter Morgan; the hit musical *Jersey Boys*; and a reboot of the successful action franchise, *Tomb Raider*.

Headington and King are partners in two other subsidiaries of GK Films— GK-TV and FilmDistrict. Headington is President and sole shareholder of Headington Resources, Inc. He is an active philanthropist, personally and through various family foundations.

PAUL KIEVE (On Set Magician) has performed internationally as an illusionist. He is best known for creating original magic illusions for West End and Broadway theater productions, including *The Lord of the Rings*, *The Invisible Man*, *Matilda*, and *Ghost: The Musical*, as well as the movie *Harry Potter and the Prisoner of Azkaban*, in which he also appears. His novel *Hocus Pocus* has been published in eleven languages and features an introduction by star pupil Daniel Radcliffe. You can visit his website at www.stageillusion.com.

GRAHAM KING (Producer) won a Best Picture Oscar as a producer on Martin Scorsese's crime drama *The Departed*. It marked King's third collaboration with Scorsese on films the famed filmmaker has directed. King produced the widely praised *The Aviator*, and was co-executive producer on Scorsese's Oscar-nominated epic drama *Gangs of New York*. In 2009, King and Scorsese collaborated a fourth time, producing *The Young Victoria*.

In 2007, Mr. King launched his independent production company GK Films with business partner Tim Headington. Since 2007, GK Films produced *Edge of Darkness* and *The Young Victoria*, among other movies. Most recently Mr. King produced *The Tourist, The Town, Rango*, and the upcoming films *The Rum Diary* and *In the Land of Blood and Honey*.

He is currently producing *Dark Shadows*; and developing the untitled Freddie Mercury story starring Sacha Baron Cohen being written by Peter Morgan; the hit musical *Jersey Boys*; and a reboot of the successful action franchise, *Tomb Raider*. King is also a partner in two other subsidiaries of GK Films— GK-TV and FilmDistrict.

A native of the United Kingdom, he moved to the United States in 1982 and was awarded an OBE (Officer of the Order of the British Empire) in 2009.

SIR BEN KINGSLEY (Georges Méliès) earned an Academy Award, as well as international fame, for his riveting portrayal of Indian social leader Mahatma

Gandhi in the movie *Gandhi*. He has since played dozens of complex and wide-ranging characters, and in the process earned three more Oscar nominations for his work on *Bugsy*, *Sexy Beast*, and *The House of Sand and Fog*. He collaborated previously with Martin Scorsese on the hit movie *Shutter Island*.

Steeped in British theater, Mr. Kingsley marked the beginning of his professional acting career with the Royal Shakespeare Company in 1967, where his roles included Othello and Hamlet. In 2001, he received a knighthood from Queen Elizabeth.

JUDE LAW (Hugo's Father), two-time Oscar nominee, is one of the most sought after talents in the acting world. He recently co-starred in the hit film *Sherlock Holmes*, playing Dr. Watson. Mr. Law, who was born in London and appeared with Britain's National Youth Music Theater at age twelve, first attracted attention with his appearance on stage in Jean Cocteau's *Les Parents Terribles*, which earned him a Tony nomination when he played the role on Broadway.

His other film appearances include *Wilde*, *Midnight in the Garden of Good and Evil*, *Gattaca*, *The Talented Mr. Ripley* (Academy Award nomination for Best Supporting Actor), *A.I. Artificial Intelligence*, *Road to Perdition*, *Cold Mountain* (Academy Award nomination for Best Actor), and *Closer* among many other films.

Mr. Law was recently acclaimed for his performance as Hamlet produced by the Donmar Warehouse in London's West End. He received a Tony nomination for Best Actor when he brought the show to Broadway.

SIR CHRISTOPHER LEE (Monsieur Labisse) has recently starred as Mr. Wonka, Willy's dentist father, in *Charlie and the Chocolate Factory*, and in *The Lord of the Rings* trilogy from New Line Cinema; *Star Wars: Episode II—Attack of the Clones* and *Star Wars: Episode III—Revenge of the Sith* from Lucasfilm.

Mr. Lee's legendary career spans more than sixty years and two hundred and seventy movies, amongst which a few of the best known are *Dracula*, *The Mummy*, *The Wicker Man*, *The Man with the Golden Gun* (based on the book written by his cousin Ian Fleming), *Airport '77*, *Jinnah*, *Gremlins II*, as well as Tim Burton's *Sleepy Hollow* and *Corpse Bride*.

He considers the most important point in his career to have been as host of *Saturday Night Live* in 1978. The directors for whom he has worked include John Huston, Orson Welles, Nicholas Ray, Michael Powell, and Billy Wilder.

In 2001, Mr. Lee was made Commander of the Order of the British Empire, and in 2009 received a knighthood from Queen Elizabeth.

ROB LEGATO (Second Unit Director and Visual Effects Supervisor) received a Masters Degree in Cinematography from Brooks Institute of Photography in Santa Barbara, California, and began working as a live action commercial producer, visual effects supervisor, and director for visual effects-oriented TV spots. He served as alternating visual effects supervisor for the TV series *Twilight Zone* and was visual effects supervisor and second unit and episode director for *Star Trek: The Next Generation*, as well as visual effects supervisor for the series *Deep Space Nine*. Mr. Legato then joined Digital Domain, the visual effects company founded by director James Cameron and others. His film credits include *Interview with a Vampire*, *Apollo 13* (Academy Award nomination), James Cameron's *Titanic* (Academy Award), *Harry Potter and The Sorcerer's Stone*, *The Good Shepherd*, *Avatar*, and Scorsese's *Kundun*, *The Aviator*, *The Departed*, *Shine a Light*, and *Shutter Island*.

ELLEN LEWIS (Casting Director) has worked with Martin Scorsese since *New York Stories* in 1989 and has cast all his subsequent films. She's also cast such movies as *Forrest Gump*, *Wit*, *Angels in America*, *Broken Flowers*, *The Devil Wears Prada*, *Before the Devil Knows You're Dead*, *Charlotte's Web*, and *Mamma Mia!*

FRANCESCA LO SCHIAVO (Set Decorator) has collaborated with her husband Dante Ferretti and Martin Scorsese for many years. Among her numerous other credits are Franco Zeffirelli's *Hamlet*, Terry Gilliam's *Baron Munchausen*, and Federico Fellini's *And the Ship Sails On*.

JOHN LOGAN (Screenwriter) previously collaborated with Martin Scorsese on *The Aviator*, earning an Academy Award nomination for his screenplay. He also earned an Oscar nomination for his script of the Oscar-winning film *Gladiator*. Among notable films written by Mr. Logan are *Any Given Sunday*, the TV movie *RKO 281*, *Star Trek: Nemesis*, *The Time Machine*, and *Sweeney Todd: The Demon Barber of Fleet Street*. He recently adapted Shakespeare's *Coriolanus* for the screen in which Ralph Fiennes starred and directed. He has also written the script for the next James Bond movie, directed by Sam Mendes.

In 2010, Mr. Logan's play *Red* was performed at the Donmar Warehouse in London and on Broadway, winning the Tony Award for Best Play.

LARRY McCONKEY (Steadicam Operator), who was born in Iowa City, has worked on over 125 movies. Mr. McConkey attended Cornell University, majoring in cinema, and also received an MFA from Temple University in documentary film. His many film credits include *Eat Pray Love*, *American Gangster*, *The Good Shepherd*, *Interview with a Vampire*, *Quiz Show*, *George Balanchine's The Nutcracker*, *The Silence of the Lambs*, *The Untouchables*, *Broadcast News*, and Scorsese's *Goodfellas* and *Bringing Out the Dead*.

HELEN McCRORY (Mama Jeanne) is best known to screen audiences from her appearances as Narcissa Malfoy in *Harry Potter and The Deathly Hallows* (Parts 1 and 2) and *Harry Potter and the Half-Blood Prince*. She also portrayed Cherie Blair, the British Prime Minister's wife, in two different films, *The Special Relationship* and *The Queen*. Ms. McCrory began her career at the National Theatre in London, playing leading roles in *Blood Wedding* and *The Seagull*. Among her other film credits are *The Count of Monte Cristo*, *Interview with a Vampire*, and *Becoming Jane*. In addition, she voiced the character of Mrs. Bean in *Fantastic Mr. Fox*.

TIM MONICH (Dialect Coach) has over thirty-five years experience in theater and film. Having trained with Edith Skinner at Carnegie Mellon University, he was on the faculty of the Juilliard School for twelve years. His 135 feature film projects include *A Dry White Season*, *Thelma and Louise*, *Schindler's List*, *JFK*, *Six Degrees of Separation*, *Quiz Show*, *The Talented Mr. Ripley*, *Dead Man*

Walking, Cold Mountain, Ali, The Aviator, Million Dollar Baby, and True Grit. Hugo is his seventh collaboration with Martin Scorsese. Mr. Monich was the subject of a November 2009 profile in The New Yorker.

CHLOË MORETZ (Isabelle) made her first professional appearance at the age of seven in two episodes of the TV series The Guardian. She then made her feature film debut in Heart of the Beholder, which was followed by a role in The Amityville Horror. Since then she has appeared in many movies including (500) Days of Summer, Diary of a Wimpy Kid, and Let Me In, where she played a child vampire. On TV, Chloë has appeared on My Name Is Earl, Desperate Housewives, and 30 Rock. She'll soon appear in The Devil and the Deep Blue Sea, Hick, and Tim Burton's Dark Shadows.

EMILY MORTIMER (Lisette) had her breakout performance in Lovely & Amazing, and went on to appear in such movies as Match Point, The Pink Panther, Dear Frankie, Martin Scorsese's Shutter Island, and Lars and the Real Girl. Her theater works include the world premiere of Jez Butterworth's Parlour Song, and The Merchant of Venice for the Lyceum Theatre.
　　Born in London, she is the daughter of lawyer/playwright Sir John Mortimer and Penelope Gallop. Ms. Mortimer attended St. Paul's School and Oxford University where she studied English and Russian.

MARTHA PINSON (Script Supervisor) met Martin Scorsese while he was filming the Michael Jackson video Bad. They have since worked together on Shutter Island, The Departed, The Aviator, Bringing Out the Dead, and New York Stories. She's also worked on movies ranging from Prince of the City, Night Falls on Manhattan, and A Stranger Among Us, to Deathtrap, Ragtime, Wall Street, and Dressed to Kill. She graduated with Honors from Vassar College with a Major in English and a specialization in Shakespeare.

DEMETRI PORTELLI (3-D Stereographer) began his film career as a young director of music videos and a series of TV commercials, as well as several documentary-style TV series. His credits include the TV series Soul Food, Warehouse 13, Aaron Stone, and Wild Card. The Virgin Suicides, Resident Evil: Apocalypse and Resident Evil: Aftermath, Anne of Green Gables, Grace, How She Move, Casino Jack, and Collaborator are among his feature film credits.

SANDY POWELL (Costume Designer) has worked with Martin Scorsese on Gangs of New York, The Departed, Shutter Island, and The Aviator, for which she won an Oscar. She also won Oscars for her designs for Shakespeare in Love and Young Victoria.
　　Her other credits include Velvet Goldmine, The Tempest, Far from Heaven, Caravaggio, The Last of England, The Crying Game, and Orlando. On stage, Ms. Powell has designed costumes for many plays and operas, including A Midsummer Night's Dream, Nijinsky, Rigoletto, and Edward II.

ROBERT RICHARDSON (Cinematographer) is a two-time Academy Award winner, for Oliver Stone's JFK and Martin Scorsese's The Aviator. His other collaborations with Scorsese include *Casino*, *Bringing Out the Dead*, and *Shutter Island*. Most recently, he led the team of star cinematographers who filmed Scorsese's Rolling Stones documentary *Shine a Light*.

Mr. Richardson attended the Rhode Island School of Design as well as the American Film Institute. His other notable movies include *Platoon*, *Wall Street*, *Nixon*, *Eight Men Out*, *A Few Good Men*, *The Horse Whisperer*, *Kill Bill* (Volumes 1 and 2), *Inglourious Basterds*, and *Eat Pray Love*.

MORAG ROSS (Makeup Designer) was born in Glasgow, Scotland, and studied Mural Design at Glasgow School of Art. She trained as a makeup artist with the BBC in London, and has worked in the film industry for over twenty years, receiving three BAFTA awards, and working with many directors, including Steven Spielberg, Ang Lee, Todd Haynes, and Martin Scorsese.

THELMA SCHOONMAKER (Editor) edited Martin Scorsese's first feature film, *Who's That Knocking at My Door?* She then edited a series of films and commercials before supervising the editing of the 1971 documentary *Woodstock*, for which she was nominated for an Academy Award.

Ms. Schoonmaker is a three-time Academy Award winner, having been honored for Scorsese's *The Departed*, *The Aviator*, and *Raging Bull*. Since *Raging Bull* in 1980, she has worked on all of Scorsese's features. She also edited his documentary *A Personal Journey with Martin Scorsese Through American Movies*, and his documentary about Italian cinema, *Il Mio Viaggio in Italia*.

In addition to her film editing, she works tirelessly to promote the films and writings of her late husband, the director Michael Powell, whose classic *The Red Shoes* had so enthralled her as a girl.

MARTIN SCORSESE (Director) was born in New York City in 1942. He studied film communications at New York University's School of Film, and in 1968, directed his first feature film, *Who's That Knocking at My Door?* He won critical and popular acclaim for his 1973 film *Mean Streets*, which was followed by his first documentary, *Italianamerican*, in 1974, as well as the feature *Alice Doesn't Live Here Anymore*.

In 1976, Mr. Scorsese's *Taxi Driver* was awarded the Palme d'Or at the Cannes Film Festival. In 1980, *Raging Bull*, which many consider to be one of the best movies ever made, received eight Academy Award nominations, including Best Picture and Best Director. Mr. Scorsese's movies after this include *The King of Comedy*, *Goodfellas*, and *The Age of Innocence*.

His long-cherished project *Gangs of New York* was released in 2002, earning numerous critical honors, including a Golden Globe Award for Best Director. In 2004, *The Aviator* earned five Academy Awards. His film *The Departed* was released to critical acclaim in 2006, earning four Academy Awards, including Best Picture and Best Director. *Shutter Island* was released in 2010 and was a huge box office success.

Mr. Scorsese is the founder and chair of the Film Foundation, a non-profit organization dedicated to the preservation and protection of motion picture history. Check out their website at www.film-foundation.org.

BRIAN SELZNICK (Author/Artist) was working at Eeyore's Books for Children in Manhattan when his first book, *The Houdini Box*, was published. He has now illustrated and/or written over twenty books for children, including *Frindle* by Andrew Clements and *The Dinosaurs of Waterhouse Hawkins* by Barbara Kerley, which received a Caldecott Honor. *The Invention of Hugo Cabret* was a number one *New York Times* bestseller, a National Book Award finalist, and the winner of the 2008 Caldecott Medal, among other distinctions.

DAVID SERLIN (Writer/Historian) is a writer, historian, and professor of communication at the University of California, San Diego. He has published many books and articles on American culture, technology, and media. He is currently completing a book about how people with disabilities experience city life entitled *Window Shopping with Helen Keller*.

HOWARD SHORE (Composer) is among today's most respected, honored, and active composers and music conductors. His work with Peter Jackson on *The Lord of the Rings* trilogy stands as a towering achievement, earning him three Academy Awards, four Grammys, and three Golden Globes. Mr. Shore was one of the original creators of *Saturday Night Live*, serving as music director from 1975 to 1980. He has scored thirteen films by David Cronenberg including *The Fly*, *Dead Ringers*, *Naked Lunch*, and *Eastern Promises*. He has collaborated with Martin Scorsese on *The Departed*, *The Aviator*, *Gangs of New York*, and *After Hours*. Other films include *Ed Wood*, *The Silence of the Lambs*, and *Mrs. Doubtfire*. His opera, *The Fly*, had its world premiere in 2008 in Paris and its U.S. premiere at LA Opera.

MICHAEL STUHLBARG (René Tabard) first became known to film audiences in 2009 for his highly acclaimed leading performance in the Coen brothers' film *A Serious Man*. Stuhlbarg's other film appearances include *Afterschool*, *Body of Lies*, *Cold Souls*, and *The Grey Zone*. He is currently filming *Men in Black III* with Barry Sonnenfeld. He appeared in Martin Scorsese's short film *The Key to Reserva*, and is in his second season of HBO's *Boardwalk Empire*, which Scorsese executive produced, in addition to directing the pilot episode. He attended UCLA and trained at the Juilliard School in New York. His numerous theatrical appearances include *The Pillowman*, which earned him a Tony Award nomination, the title character in *Hamlet* at the Public Theater, and *The Voysey Inheritance*, for which he received an Obie Award.

CHRIS SURGENT (First Assistant Director) graduated from Lehigh University in 1988 and was accepted into the Directors Guild of America's Assistant Directors' training program, graduating in 1996. He has since been working as an assistant director in film and television. He has worked with Martin Scorsese on *Gangs of New York*, *Bringing Out the Dead*, *Casino*, *The Aviator*, and *Boardwalk Empire*. Other projects include *I Am Legend*, *Gone Baby Gone*, and *Mona Lisa Smile*.

JOSS WILLIAMS (Special Effects) began his career as a special effects technician on *Superman I* and *II*, *Octopussy*, *Indiana Jones and the Temple of Doom*, *Air America*, and *Patriot Games*. In 1989, Joss became special effects supervisor on *Son of the Pink Panther*. At the same time, he founded the special effects company Darkside FX, based at Pinewood Studios. Joss's more recent credits as FX supervisor are *In the Name of the Father, Hamlet, Sleepy Hollow, Charlie and the Chocolate Factory, Munich, United 93, Elizabeth: the Golden Age, The Bourne Ultimatum* (BAFTA nomination), *Green Zone*, and HBO's series *The Pacific*. In 2008, he established The Special Effects Training Company with Darkside FX.

RAY WINSTONE (Uncle Claude) studied acting at the Corona School before being cast in his first TV series. After playing a starring role in *Quadrophenia*, he played the lead in *Nil by Mouth* to great acclaim. His other film credits include *Sexy Beast, Ripley's Game, Cold Mountain, King Arthur, The Proposition, Beowulf, Indiana Jones and the Kingdom of the Crystal Skull, Percy Jackson*, and Martin Scorsese's *The Departed*.

Thank You To . . .

Martin Scorsese, and the cast and crew of *Hugo* who made this book possible, with a special nod to Marianne Bower for all her help; Graham King and everyone at GK Films, including Grey Rembert. Thanks also to Tamazin Simmons; Jason Dravis; Noel Silverman; David Serlin; John Gaughan; Jane Claire Quigley; the staff at New Deal Studios who invited David Serlin and me to LA to watch the miniature train crash; Logan Boettcher; Anna Armatis and Kyle Cummings from Film Solutions, LLC; Michael Start; Ben Grossmann; Charles Kreloff; the staff at Scholastic, especially Tracy Mack, David Saylor, Emellia Zamani, Veronica Ambrose, Elizabeth Mayo, Els Rijper, Ellie Berger, Lori Benton, Karyn Browne, Joanna Croteau, and Joseph Romano.

Thank you to Larry Kaplan, publicist extraordinaire, for the ceaseless work he did to help bring this book to life, from coordinating all the interviews, to acting as the perfect liaison between myself and everyone involved in the movie, to filling in all the blanks about the process and details that went into creating this film. His work on this book was heroic.

And finally, this book would not exist without the support, collaboration, and constant input of Helen Scorsese. It was her singular vision and determination that guided us as we created *The Hugo Movie Companion*.

Photo Credits and Permissions

Page 8: Jacket art for *The Invention of Hugo Cabret* copyright © 2007 by Brian Selznick. Pages 10-11: Still from *Le voyage dans la lune (A Trip to the Moon)*, 1902, Georges Méliès. From the collection of the British Film Institute. Pages 14-15, 16-17, 18-19, 74-75, 90-91, 102-103, 140-141, 142-143, 146-147, 152-153: Brian Selznick's drawings from *The Invention of Hugo Cabret* copyright © 2007 by Brian Selznick. Pages 22-23: Photographs courtesy of Brian Selznick. Pages 24, 26-27: *A view of the Eiffel Tower, Paris, from the top of the Arc de Triomphe.* Francis M. R. Hudson/Topical Press Agency/Getty Images. Page 32: Scorsese family photo, courtesy of the collection of Martin Scorsese. Page 33: *Duel in the Sun*, 1946, directed by King Vidor, Selznick Releasing/Photofest. Page 46: Auguste (left) and Louis Lumière. SSPL via Getty Images. Page 47: Still from *L'Eclipse du soleil en pleine lune (The Eclipse)*, 1907, Georges Méliès. From the collection of the British Film Institute. Page 48 top: Still from *L'Arriveé d'un train á La Ciotat (Arrival of a Train at La Ciotat)*, 1895, Auguste and Louis Lumière. Photofest. Page 48 bottom: Still from *Sous les toits de Paris (Under the Roofs of Paris)*, 1930, René Clair. Films Sonores Tobis/Photofest. Page 49 top: Still from *La belle et la bête (Beauty and the Beast)*, 1946, Jean Cocteau. Lopert Pictures Corporation/Photofest. Page 49 bottom: Still from *Les quatre cents coups (The 400 Blows)*, 1959, François Truffaut. Archives du 7e Art/DR/Photo12/The Image Works. Page 52 top left: Police station at the corner of rue de la Huchette and rue du Chat-qui-Peche, ca. 1930. Silver gelatin print. Brassaï (Gyula Halasz, called, 1899-1984) © Estate Brassaï-RMN. Location: Musée National d'Art Moderne, Centre Georges Pompidou, Paris, France. Photo Credit: CNAC/MNAM/Dist. Réunion des Musées Nationaux / Art Resource, NY. Page 52 top right: Woman on a corner, rue Quincampoix, ca. 1932. Silver gelatin print. Brassaï (Gyula Halasz, called, 1899-1984) © Estate Brassaï- RMN Location: Musée National d'Art Moderne, Centre Georges Pompidou, Paris, France. Photo Credit: CNAC/MNAM/Dist. Réunion des Musées Nationaux/Art Resource, NY. Page 52 bottom: Bistro, Paris, 1927, André Kertész. © Estate of André Kertész/Higher Pictures. Page 56 bottom: Diagram of visual effect with aquarium and mermaid from book title *Georges Méliès Mage* by Maurice Bessy and Lo Duca, 1945 from the collection of La Cinémathèque Française. Pages 63 and 209: Screenplay copyright © 2010 GK Films LLC. All rights reserved. Page 82: Portrait of Georges Méliès, 1921 Albert Harlingue/Roger-Viollet/The Image Works. Pages 84-85: Georges Méliès in his shop at the Montparnasse train station, undated from the collection of La Cinémathèque Française. Pages 140, 141, 144-145: Train station model, floor plan of train station, and secret apartment sketch courtesy of Dante Ferretti. Pages 156-157: Blueprint of the automaton courtesy of David Balfour. Page 158: *Mona Lisa*, (portrait of Lisa del Giocondo) painting by Leonardo da Vinci. © Louvre, Paris, France, photographer Stuart Dee/Photographer's Choice/Getty Images. Page 162: Vichy Acrobat, Michael Start, The House of Automata. Page 164: Antonio Diavolo, John Gaughan collection. Page 165 top right: Magician, Michael Start, The House of Automata. Page 165 top left: Henri Maillardet Automaton, Franklin Institute. Page 165 bottom: Automaton duck, automaton of Jacques de Vaucanson (1709-1782), French engineer. Albert Harlingue/Roger-Viollet/The Image Works. Pages 168-169: Costume sketches courtesy of Sandy Powell. Pages 188-189: Train crash on film location © Logan Boettcher/New Deal Studios. Page 197: Tim Monich's pronunciation page courtesy of Tim Monich. Page 209: Martha Pinson's script notations courtesy of Martha Pinson. Page 217: Howard Shore's musical score page courtesy of Howard Shore, © 2011 South Fifth Avenue Publishing, (ASCAP). Pages 232-233: Storyboards for the party scene courtesy of Martin Scorsese.